THE
MOTHER'S
FAULT

BOOKS BY NICOLE TROPE

My Daughter's Secret
The Boy in the Photo
The Nowhere Girl
The Life She Left Behind
The Girl Who Never Came Home
Bring Him Home
The Family Across the Street

NICOLE TROPE

THE MOTHER'S FAULT

bookouture

She should have broken it off earlier, but she was seduced by his smile and the way he held her hand, and the nice dinners out where he insisted on paying for the babysitter. *What's done is done.*

She unlocks the car while Riley checks the timber mailbox. It's painted red and has a chicken on top of it. She and Riley bought it together and he thinks it's hilarious.

Every morning, before they leave for school, he opens the mailbox despite knowing that the mail comes in the afternoon. She slides into the car and waits for him to get in and tell her, 'Nothing yet,' as he does every morning.

'You won't believe it, you won't believe it,' he says excitedly, flinging open the door and jumping into the car. 'It's a present and it's for me. It has a card and everything and it's not even my birthday,' he shouts, his eyes shining with delight.

'What?' Beverly asks, turning around to see him holding a small square box. 'Give me that.'

'But it's for me,' he protests, 'for me.'

'Riley, let me look at it please,' she says, her voice stern. Right now, the stern voice works to a certain extent, but she's not sure how long that will last for. How will she discipline him if he grows to over six foot, as she assumes he will do? His father was over six foot.

'Fine,' he says, reluctantly handing her the box.

She turns it over in her hand. The wrapping paper is blue with silver stars. She gives it a shake and then for some reason she sniffs it. 'I'm just going to read the card first,' she says.

'But it's for me,' he shouts.

'Yes, but I need to know who it's from,' she says back, louder than she means to, and then she takes a deep breath, calming herself. He is getting more and more difficult to manage and she worries all the time now about who he will be one day, who he will become. Sometimes she types his behaviours into Google and terrifies herself with all the diagnoses the internet spits at her.

That's something else she does late at night with a glass of wine and it never leads anywhere good.

The card is small and placed inside a blue envelope. She slides it out and reads the note. It's been written on a computer and printed:

Dear Riley
Thought you might enjoy this.

It says nothing else.

'Give it to me, give it to me,' shouts Riley giving the back of her seat an enormous kick.

'You stop that right now, young man, stop it now,' she reprimands him, but she hands him the box and watches him open it.

It's a handball, half black, half white. The white part has a sun painted on it and the black part has the moon and stars. 'Cool,' he says. 'I can play with it at school today.'

Beverly nods. 'Yes, I guess.' It's harmless, just a present. No need for her to worry, she tells herself, although she has no idea who it could be from.

Her phone pings with a text. *We need to talk.* She's never thought of Ethan as manipulative, but he's obviously decided that he can get to her through Riley. She contemplates taking the present away but doesn't have the energy for the argument that would ensue.

'Just leave me alone,' Beverly mutters to her phone. She reverses the car and pulls out into the street so she can get Riley to school.

The gift is probably from Ethan. They had almost been a little family and she knows that he loves Riley. But she cannot have him in their lives. She just knows that she cannot allow him to move her and Riley somewhere new, and to let him begin taking over and taking care of them because there is always the possibility of things falling apart, of the truth seeping out and the consequences of that. Never mind how difficult marriage can be anyway. A marriage begun on secrets has little hope of succeeding.

She and Riley have managed, just the two of them, for this long. They'll manage until he's independent. It feels like she has to do this alone, like it's a debt that is owed. There is always the worry that if she does agree to being with a man, together forever, and then something changes, Riley will get caught between the two of them. That happened to him once when he was too young to know about it, too young to know that it nearly cost him his life. People who love each other can so easily turn into people who loathe each other. No one ever thinks it will happen to them. But anything is possible. She knows that more than most.

'Who's it from, do you think?' Riley asks.

'I don't know,' she says, because she's not totally sure and if Ethan's chosen not to sign his name, maybe he doesn't want a thank you. If she calls him and asks if he wants a thank you then they will end up having the same conversation over again. Maybe it was a 'goodbye' gift from him.

'Doesn't matter, I love it,' Riley says. 'I love it.'

CHAPTER TWO
Riley

'Do you know,' says Riley as he threads his legs through the monkey bars and hangs upside down, 'that the world record for the longest handball game is seventy hours?' He is holding his new handball while he and Benji wait their turn on the court. Two of the older boys are playing now and once they finish, Mrs Edwards, the playground teacher on duty, has assured them it will be their turn. Riley is watching the game even as he hangs upside down, making sure that the moment one of them is out, he and Benji get their turn. Older boys can be sneaky sometimes and sneakiness makes Riley so, so angry.

'Where'd you hear that?' asks Benji. He is sitting on top of the monkey bars, also keeping an eye on the handball game in progress. 'If they don't finish soon, recess will be over.'

'We can play at lunch,' says Riley, 'and I read it on the internet.'

'What do you think of Mr Benton?' asks Benji, referring to their new teacher.

'I think he's good, he's really tall.'

'Yeah,' agrees Benji. 'One day we'll be that tall, although my dad is kind of short. Was your dad tall?'

Riley swings himself up to catch the bars and rights himself after stuffing the ball in his pocket. 'My mum said he was.'

'Does it make you really sad, you know, not having a dad?' Benji picks at a scab on his knee. He's doing it slowly so it doesn't bleed.

Riley thinks about this for a moment. 'Sometimes,' he says and then he shrugs. 'Sometimes I pretend that he's not dead but somewhere else, you know, like living overseas, and one day he'll come and get me and then Mum will be happy all the time and I'll be happy all the time, but I know it's just pretend.'

'Maybe not,' says Benji excitedly, 'maybe he's alive and he's like a spy and so your mum can't tell you and maybe he sent you the handball.' Benji is the best story writer in the class. He always gets an A.

'Wow, cool,' says Riley as he thinks about this. It's possible because anything is possible. He hangs from the monkey bars, letting his arms stretch as he imagines a tall man with brown hair and big muscles, listening through an earpiece to some people he's spying on. 'I bet my dad is as tall as Mr Benton.'

'Probably,' says Benji. 'Spies need to be tall and have big muscles. Ask your mum, she's seen him.'

Riley drops down from the monkey bars. His mum has no pictures of his dad at all, absolutely none. 'They were in a box and got lost when we moved into this house,' she has told him. Riley doesn't understand exactly how that's possible since all the other pictures of him as a baby, of his mother, his uncle and his grandparents, are still around.

'I wish I knew what he looked like,' says Riley. 'Even though my mum has told me, it's not the same as seeing a picture.'

'Guess not. Maybe you should google him, like put his name in and look him up.'

'I tried that,' says Riley as he drops onto the ground. He shoves his hand into his pocket, feeling the smooth rubber of the ball, 'but there were like hundreds of people with the same name and my mum said it wasn't any of them.' He had typed John Paul Jackson into Google as she watched him, even though she kept saying, 'He won't be there.' She was right about that. 'Not everyone has an internet presence, Riley,' she had told him.

It's weird that there's nothing there. If Riley types his name into Google, his mum's Facebook page comes up because she sometimes puts pictures of him on there. He's only a kid and he's already on the internet. How come his father isn't there at all? He wants to push his mother, to ask her questions until he gets an answer that makes sense, but any time they talk about his dad she looks so sad that he feels bad for her.

Riley takes the handball out of his pocket, studying it. 'Do you really think this could be from my dad?' he asks Benji.

Benji shrugs. 'It would be cool if it was.'

'Yeah,' agrees Riley and when the bell rings before he and Benji get their turn on the court, he doesn't even get upset. He's too busy picturing a tall man with hair the same colour he has, placing a present into their mailbox and then hiding until he sees his son get it.

CHAPTER THREE

Here are some things I know about the old man I live with. He's eighty-one and a widower. He has a small dog named Scotty. Scotty is a black Scottish terrier which means that the old man I live with also lacks an imagination, but that suits me. His name is Sam and he is tall with a paunch and stick-like legs, blue eyes and snow-white hair. He misses his wife Marjorie and whenever he's worried about something or forgets something or is trying to make a decision, he mutters, 'WWMD?' What would Marjorie do? Marjorie died three years ago, just clutched her chest and said, 'Oh, Sam, I feel a terrible pain.' He still tells old friends this story, even though they have probably heard it many times before. But they're old as well so perhaps they don't mind hearing it again. He seems to have quite a few old friends who call regularly, which is a good thing because he lives alone and his daughter lives in Melbourne. It's nice that people check on him because age is starting to affect Sam.

Sometimes Sam forgets to feed Scotty and the little black dog will follow him around until he says, 'What do you want, Scotty boy? What are you trying to tell me?' If I am around and I see that the dog's food or water dish are empty, I tip some of his kibble in or fill up the water. I hate the idea of a dog going hungry. That's very cruel. Dogs don't understand cruelty. Humans understand it and if they don't, it can be explained to them. Although I grew up with a fair level of cruelty and even though the reasons for it were explained almost constantly, I'm still not sure I understand them all.

Sam sometimes forgets to eat but hunger usually drives him to the fridge in the middle of the night. He has a newish fridge and often leaves the door open when he returns to bed, causing an annoying beeping sound. His daughter bought him the fridge for just this reason but if he doesn't hear the beeping or just ignores the sound then I'm not sure what the point is. The fridge is an incongruous, hulking stainless-steel box in a dated kitchen filled with creaky appliances, but when his old fridge broke, he didn't even get a chance to think about what he would replace it with before his daughter had ordered something new and arranged for it to be delivered. He also tells those who call for a chat this story over and over, but I think he tells it with a reasonable level of pride in her. 'Just turned up – can you imagine? I said to the bloke, "That's not for me. I didn't order anything." And he said, "It's all paid for and I have to install it and take away the old one, and I can also help you put everything in the new one. It's all been organised." But that's my little girl for you, always looking out for her old man.'

His daughter is a lawyer, as is her husband, and they make a nice amount of money. That's what Sam calls it, 'A nice amount of money'.

Sam is still able to take care of himself to a certain extent – aside from leaving the fridge open and occasionally forgetting to feed Scotty and himself. He should be in a home, if you ask me. His daughter, Liza, asks him every night to move from Sydney to Melbourne and live with her. She calls him every single night and asks how he is and then I hear him say, 'No, Liza… I don't think Scotty would like to move and neither would I. But thank you, my love.' It's a sweet relationship and I'm pretty sure that at some point Liza will stop asking and will get on a plane and drag her father back home with her. But until that happens, he's doing okay.

He's mostly happy unless he's missing Marjorie. He likes to look at their wedding album, which is filled with black-and-white photos of the two of them dressed up in their finery. He was a handsome young man with thick dark hair and she was quite pretty with big dark eyes and light-coloured hair. She wore a floor-length dress, straight, and fitted with gloves. She had a little net veil with a sparkly comb in her hair. He was in a tux. They were a good-looking couple and Liza seems to have inherited the best of both of them. She has black hair and blue eyes and a pretty smile, really pretty. Her children look more like her husband who is overweight and balding with permanently red cheeks. Their photographs litter the house, on every available surface. Sam sometimes carries them around with him, as though taking his grandchildren into the next room. The granddaughters are six and eight. Thea plays the violin very badly. When Liza calls Sam, she makes him listen to Thea playing and the screeching sound carries through the house. Thea would do best to choose some other instrument. The other granddaughter, the six-year-old, is called Amy and she gets on the phone, says hello and then gives the phone back to her mother. Liza and the children will be up at the end of the month, in three weeks' time, to visit. I paid close attention to that call.

Sam is really looking forward to seeing them. They are going to stay in the house with him, but Liza has told Sam not to worry, she'll sort everything out when she gets here. Sam told a friend of his that Liza said this and he is quite relieved. He doesn't manage things as well as he used to. He is planning to make Marjorie's famous lemon meringue pie to welcome them all and he has made several terrible attempts, but they all still taste okay despite looking like a lemony-meringue mess with a crust that doesn't stick together. But he's happy to keep trying. 'I'm happy to keep at it until I get it right,' he told Liza. I'm not sure Liza thinks this is a good idea. She worries about him using the stove. 'Yes, the stove is off,' he tells her at the end of each phone call. He's lucky to have a daughter who loves him so much, but then he was probably a really good father when she was growing up. I did not have a good father or a good mother, but I recognise one when I see them.

Oh, and there's one other thing I know about Sam.

He doesn't know I'm here.

CHAPTER FOUR

Beverly

'Guess what, guess what, guess what?' says Riley as he sees her. His pale blue school shirt is stained with daubs of red paint and his shoelaces are undone and grubby from being stepped on.

'You had art today?' Beverly smiles.

'How did you know?' he asks, amazement in his voice.

She touches a spot of red paint. 'Didn't you wear your apron?'

'Hmm,' he says, looking down at himself. 'I did but I don't know what happened. The cleaner lady asked me the same question,' he shrugs, 'but that's not what I wanted to tell you.'

'What did you want to tell me?' she asks, taking his backpack and waiting for him to climb into the car. When he's in and she can see he's buckled his seat belt, she gets in and turns around to look at him.

'Mrs Randall broke her arm. She was on a hike with her husband, Mr Randall, and she fell and her arm went like ker-runch, and now she's at home and we have a substitute.' There is little more exciting to an eight-year-old than a broken bone. Last month Riley's friend, George, broke his wrist and was school royalty while his cast was on.

'Poor Mrs Randall,' says Beverly thinking of the tall, grey-haired year three teacher who kept her class in line with only a look. Her emails to Beverly were short and to the point: *Today I had reason to discipline Riley for talking in class during a test.*

Today Riley stayed in at lunch because he shouted out the answer to a question without raising his hand.

Today Riley went to visit the principal's office because he swore during class.

Beverly sighs each time she sees the teacher's email address pop up. But she knows that Mrs Randall actually likes Riley because she tries hard to send good emails as well: *Today Riley behaved impeccably and received not one but two gold stars* ☺

'Yeah, and we had to write cards to her. I told her to get better soon. Benji said that he told her to get better but not too soon because Benji got into trouble for not doing his spelling last week and had to have a time out so he couldn't play at lunchtime, but he played with me today and we played handball and he thinks my new ball is way cool.'

Benji is Riley's best friend, a child who looks scraggly from the moment his mother drops him off at school. His shirt is always untucked, his blond hair always too long and he never wipes the Nutella off his face. Benji's mother, Ada, is completely relaxed about everything because she is thirty-seven and has five children and says, 'If I cared about everything, darl, I would go off my head.' As she watches her youngest three children file into the primary school, Ada takes out her one cigarette of the day and puffs luxuriously on it. Beverly likes Ada but she finds the woman's supreme confidence intimidating. She met Ada at her first mothers' group, where the older woman had helpfully pointed out that Beverly was wearing her baby sling the wrong way. Even now Beverly feels her face flame at the memory. She had to learn so much so quickly.

She realises that Riley is still talking so she tunes back in because he gets upset if she misses something important, believing that pretty much everything he says is important.

'Our substitute teacher is Mr Benton and he asked us all about our mums and dads and I told him that you're a librarian—'

'Not yet, I'm still studying,' Beverly says, although she has her doubts that she will ever finish the part-time online course she's been doing for the last four years.

'Yeah, but you work in a library, don't you?'

'I guess but… you're right, I'm a librarian.' She's not sure why she cares whether or not the substitute teacher knows she's qualified or not. She does go to work every day from 9 a.m. to 3 p.m. in the small suburban library where she shelves books and reads to the toddler group and conducts craft activities. She helps elderly readers find the books they need, advising regulars when something they may like comes in. It's not a job filled with excitement but she enjoys being there with Marie who's run the Hampden library for three decades. It means she can drop Riley off at school, pick him up and be there in the afternoons to help with homework. It also means that she is driving around in a twelve-year-old car, with many dents and a broken air conditioner, but she tries not to think about that.

'Mr Benton is a much better teacher than Mrs Randall but don't tell her I said so,' says Riley.

'I won't,' she says, biting down on her lip to keep from laughing.

'He's got like brown hair and big muscles, and he asked me to help him clean the whiteboard at lunchtime.'

'Oh,' she says, 'just you and him?'

'Yeah, but it was only—'

'Only what, Riley?' she asks, concerned now.

'Only 'cause I shoved Robbie in maths.' He says it softly, obviously contrite.

'Oh, Riley,' she sighs. 'Why did you shove Robbie?'

'He wouldn't lend me his ruler.'

'Where's your ruler?'

'Someone must have taken it from my bag,' he says. Beverly wants to drop her head onto the steering wheel and cry. A lost ruler is not a big deal. It's cheap and easy to replace but when it's combined with lost hats and lost jumpers and lost textbooks, it feels like just one more thing. There is no point in shouting at him or lecturing him. He'll just switch off. Riley gets his absent-mindedness from his father who she remembers lost his wallet and his keys and his caps regularly. She allows herself a small smile as she thinks of him, but this is followed by a wave of sadness that forces her to grip the steering wheel tightly enough to tense the muscles in her arms so that she doesn't give in to tears. 'There is no statute of limitations on grief,' she had once heard some psychologist say on a podcast about loss. 'And grief can come from the loss of a loved one, from the loss of a pet, from a break-up or even from the loss of a job. Your grief is your grief. Don't let anyone else dictate to you how you should feel.'

It was true. Nearly eight years now and her heartbreak felt like it would never heal.

'Shoving is not acceptable,' she says, instead of thinking anymore. Every time he does something like this, she reminds him it's not the way to react and every time he does it, she worries that it is the start of something that will lead to other behaviours that she will not be able to lecture him out of.

'I know, that's what Mr Benton said. He said that even though he's big and strong, he never hurts anyone, and I told him that you said I shouldn't hurt other people and he asked all about you and I told him you didn't have a boyfriend anymore because… Why don't you have a boyfriend anymore? Did Ethan shove you?'

'No, no of course not… we just… It's complicated, Riley.' Beverly has tried to explain why she and Ethan broke up, but an eight-year-old boy cannot understand any explanations that she can give him, especially since most of her explanations are lies anyway. She had tried saying things like, 'We weren't right for each other. Adults sometimes fight just like you and Benji fight but we couldn't make friends again. It's better if it's just you and me for now,' but she could see Riley was sceptical about everything she said. Ethan was nice to him so he didn't see why Ethan couldn't be in his life.

'Right, we're home,' she says, pulling into the driveway. 'What do you want for an afternoon snack?' she asks, hoping to distract him.

'That's what Mr Benton said as well. He said adults' lives were complicated and sometimes they make choices that kids don't understand.'

He slides out of the car and goes to check the mailbox, returning to her as she opens the door with a collection of bills that make her heart sink.

'Mr Benton said that it must be hard for you to be raising me all alone. Is it hard for you, Mum?' he asks, uncertainty forcing him to look at the ground instead of her.

Beverly stands up straight. 'Mr Benton doesn't know anything about me, Riley. I love being your mum. It's the best thing in the world.' She touches his chin so he looks up at her and grins.

'Also, I forgot to tell you that Benji knocked over a whole can of red paint that wasn't supposed to be opened but it was, and it went everywhere and the cleaner lady had to come and clean it all up and Benji had to help and I helped too and she said that I'm a nice boy.'

'You are a nice boy, you're a lovely boy,' she says, dropping a kiss on top of his head, her eyes shutting briefly as she inhales the smell of baby shampoo that he still uses to wash his hair.

He smiles again. 'I want apple and peanut butter for snack.'

'Okay,' she says and then she shivers as a cool wind bounces around a collection of leaves lying in her neglected back garden. She will need to make sure the old gas heater is working so that they can get through the freezing cold nights that are creeping closer. Ethan had wanted to buy a new house with her in a nice suburb close to the beach, but Beverly didn't want to live near the beach. The ocean with its unpredictability terrified her. She knew what could happen in the ocean. She preferred to be surrounded by trees.

CHAPTER FIVE

Sam is on the phone to Liza upstairs. I could get closer and listen to what he's saying but I'm sure it's more of the same. I find the soft murmur of his voice comforting, the way I imagine Liza once found it comforting to lie in bed and listen to her parents talk. I imagine they would have been the kind of married couple who never ran out of things to say to each other.

My parents preferred silence. Silence, or arguments that led to anxiety, and I would lie awake in my bed, chewing my fingernails, waiting for the fight to be done. *You always… You never… I can't stand it. I can't stand you.* I was always worried that they would get divorced. Not because I didn't want to come from a broken home but because I had a couple of friends with divorced parents and one of them lived with his mother and another lived with her father. I had a feeling that if there was a choice to be made, neither of my parents would want me. I was, I knew, inherently unlovable.

My parents were, as they put it, 'cursed' with two children. They were older when they had me, older still when they had my sister. I think I was a shock to the system of my forty-year-old mother. I don't know if she'd given up hope of falling pregnant or if she had never wanted children in the first place. But I do know that actually having a child made her certain that she didn't want another one and then the arrival of my sister made her hate her life. She could have ended her pregnancies or she could have given us up for adoption, I suppose, but what would people have thought? She worried a lot about what people thought, making sure that both my sister and I understood that we were a projection of her and my father. She hated us and my father hated her and the two of us. But out in public, his smile was wide enough for people to see the cracked tooth at the back of his mouth. He would push back his shoulders and hitch up his pants over his bulging stomach, nodding his balding head when people complimented him and my mother about something to do with my sister. They only ever complimented my sister. I was an ungainly, unattractive child, not a baby that people smiled at and, according to my mother, 'you were always crying'. I imagine I was left to cry a lot. My mother favoured sticking her babies in the laundry room, closing the door and leaving us to scream until we wore ourselves out into sleep.

My sister was born fourteen months after I was, so I can imagine my mother's horror at having two children under two. She handed out slaps and pinched arms and twisted ears the way other mothers handed out kisses and cuddles. My father handed out 'beltings', which involved him taking his belt out of his pants, slowly enough for the tension to build and fear to prickle all over your body. And then he used it – more on me than my sister. She was light on her feet, clever with her words and she swerved and ducked and got out of more beltings than she got. I was too slow, too stupid, too everything, and there would be weeks when I was belted every single day.

I never had a day when I looked at my mother or my father and saw love and adoration reflected back at me. They didn't love or adore my sister either, but they did respect her ability to make her way in the world: from a gurgling baby to a smiling toddler to a delicate, fairy-like little girl.

She did everything better than I did. Where I scooted around on my bum, she crawled at lightning speed. I took slow ponderous steps and still knocked my head on every table and corner I could find. My sister was an early walker, an early talker, pretty enough to make people stop in the street, and gifted according to every teacher she ever had.

But she was also raised by my parents which meant she was never very nice. Neither of us were. In a house filled with stretched, tense silences, regular beating and copious amounts of vitriol, you would think that my sister and I would have turned to each other for comfort. But instead of relying on each other as normal siblings would, we turned against each other in the hope of finding favour with people who had no desire to have us in their lives. I believe my mother knew from very early on that we were desperate for her approval and attention, and sometimes she would gift it to one of us. My sister would come home with a report card with a clean row of A's and my mother would say, 'Now that makes it all worthwhile, doesn't it?' and she would smile, her teeth slightly crooked and yellowed from many years of smoking, only given up when she got pregnant with me because the smell made her sick. It was never clear if she meant that my sister's hard work had paid off or if she was actually congratulating herself for still mothering when she had no desire to mother. And my sister would throw me a look, a smug 'see how much better I am than you' look, and I would hate her in a kind of sick, clenched way.

Abused children struggle to see their parents as the problem until they are older. Instead, they see themselves as damaged and terrible and the reason for the abuse. When my father smiled and took his belt off because I'd screwed up, I thought I deserved to be hit because I was an awful human being. If I had been better, my parents wouldn't have to hurt me. That theory only fell apart when it came to my sister because she was better but she still got hurt, even if it wasn't as much as I did. I think it helped that she looked like my mother as a girl, with brown hair and wide green eyes. There is a picture of my parents at a beach somewhere, dressed in swimsuits, and they were a beautiful couple. Her legs are long and slim, and her hair is a puffed-up brown bouffant, even on the

CHAPTER EIGHT

At the bottom of Sam's garden there is a line of green shrubs, around six feet tall. They are trimmed into a neat hedge by the gardener who comes once a month. I know he comes once a month because there is a list on Sam's fridge of things he needs to remember:

1. Take your pills after breakfast.
2. Paul comes once a month to do the garden.
3. Scotty needs his tick and flea treatment once a month.

The list is twenty points long and was made by Liza for her father. Sam reads it before he goes to bed and every night he says to Scotty, 'Nothing to remember for tomorrow except my pills, old boy.'

The tall, neat hedging at the bottom of Sam's garden is the perfect hiding spot for watching her house, and ultimately for watching him, because that's who I'm here to see. It's a little cold but I'm wearing my brown parka so I can stay here until he goes inside. He spends the afternoons in a large tree and I can see that today he climbed up there with a backpack that held his iPad and a book and something to eat – I think it's a small packet of chips. He swore when he dropped one and it fell onto the ground below the tree. The tree has very few leaves left; most having fallen on the ground creating a kind of sludgy brown mess. I can smell the damp rotting-leaf smell all over this neighbourhood. It's not a terrible smell but it makes me sad that summer is so far away again. I prefer summer, especially in Melbourne where I was until a year ago. Winter in Melbourne is icy-cold; I can never get warm enough and I'm always worried about paying for electricity, so I try not to turn on my heater too much. I suppose if I hadn't spent six years of my life wandering around Europe, I would be in a better position than I am now. But I had to leave Australia. I didn't tell anyone I was leaving because it happened so fast. I didn't care where I went, as long as it was far away. Luckily my passport was up to date, a flight to London was available and I had enough money to cover it. *Lucky, lucky, lucky.* But then I deserved some luck after everything that had happened.

It's getting dark and I know she's going to call him in for dinner. Sure enough, I hear her voice echo across the garden: 'Riley… dinner, Riley.' She has a pretty voice, the kind of voice that sounds like it belongs to a good singer, well-modulated and a little low.

Riley swears again, making me smile. He doesn't like to go inside, no matter how cold it is. There is a platform in the tree where he likes to sit, so he's really comfortable up there. I loved climbing trees as well when I was little. I wasn't very good at it. My climbing was slow and careful. Once I got there, though, I felt lighter than air. I loved looking out over our garden or over the park where there were a lot of good climbing trees. I liked to be alone up there, out of sight of my parents or, if I was in the park, out of sight of other kids.

I know why he likes it up there.

I used to like to climb trees as well.

CHAPTER NINE

Beverly

Wednesday

Beverly wakes with her heart racing, sure she's heard a sound in the house. She sits up in bed and peers at the window, trying to see if it's light through the slight parting of the heavy green curtains. It's still dark and when she looks at her bedside clock, she sees it's only 5 a.m. She sighs and lies back down on her pillows, knowing that there's no way she'll get back to sleep. The house is silent but she listens intently for a moment, trying to hear over her heartbeat, and finally she gets up, sliding out of bed, and turns on her bedroom light, shivering in the chilly air. She cannot remember her own bedroom ever being this cold when she was growing up, but her parents' old bedroom, where she sleeps, is larger and always feels less cosy. She still sleeps in the bed her parents used, despite not really liking the dark turned wood and tall headboard. A new bed is way down her list of things to buy for herself. It always has been.

Throwing on a fluffy blue robe, she slides her feet into matching fluffy blue slippers – Riley's Mother's Day gifts to her, bought with Marie's help. She knows she looks ridiculous in the oversized robe, but Riley's face lights up whenever he sees her wearing it and it is really warm. The house is cold because she's not running the heater overnight yet. The heater is for when they reach the point of frost-covered grass and being able to see your breath. She walks quickly through the house, checking all the rooms except Riley's room, knowing he will be curled up tightly, his arms around his knees under his thick duvet and Transformers blanket. She flicks lights on and off and even checks the linen cupboard, which is big enough for her to stand in, unsure why she's feeling so uneasy.

There's no one in the house and even though she would love a cup of coffee she knows that would be a bad idea. She returns to her room, still listening for a noise that's out of place. A loud stomping noise startles her and she clutches at her robe. There is more noise and she realises that it's possums, who can sound like people when they run across the roof.

'Silly,' she mutters to herself as the house subsides into silence again. She slides back into bed and lies in the dark, watching the window and the arrival of dawn as light begins to appear in the spaces her curtains leave. She used to do this as a child after waking up early on her birthday. She knew that her parents wouldn't stand for a 5 a.m. wake up and so she would lie in bed and wait for it to get light enough outside. Inevitably she would drift off to sleep again and then wake up to her mother holding a mug of hot chocolate and her father holding a cake and James holding all the birthday presents. Raucous, off-key singing would follow, James always pulling faces so she couldn't help giggling. Her whole family would sit down on her bed and she would blow out the candles and then they would all have an early morning slice of cake, which would be followed by her favourite breakfast. These days, she waits in bed until Riley wakes up and brings in an inexpertly wrapped present, chosen by Marie or Ellie. There's no singing or cake because all she wants in the morning is coffee, but none of that matters. His cards are what she looks forward to. They have grown from a few badly spelled lines to long lists of all the ways she is a good mother. *I like that you make the best spagetti in the hole world and you allways let me use as much Parmasan cheese on it as I want to. I like that you let me take my iPad up to the top of my tree. I like that you help me with my spelling.* They are her most treasured possessions.

She bites down on her lip as she thinks of her brother, James, whose curly hair was always unruly, his brown eyes always filled with light and joy. *I miss you.* Growing up, she used to make up stories of arguments she had with her older brother just to feel included in the discussions her friends had about how irritating their siblings could be. 'He just comes into my room without asking and takes my pens. He's always telling my mum she needs to be stricter with me.' But none of it was ever true. James was ten years older than she was and he had always treated her the same way her parents had, as a wonderful miracle that no one ever expected. She arrived after many years of heartbreaking miscarriages for her mother.

'At first I thought I had the flu,' her mother Orla used to tell her when she was little. She loved hearing the story of how her mother found out she was pregnant. 'But I was just so tired and James was nine already and he was such a good boy. I only did the books for Dad's plumbing business so I should have been filled with energy. But I slept and slept until Dad said—'

Beverly would chime in then, imitating her father's gravelly voice from his years as a smoker, '"Orla, this needs to stop – off to the doctor you go."'

'Well, imagine my surprise when Dr Baum suggested a pregnancy test. "I'm nearly forty," I told him, but it was positive and I cried and cried because I thought I would lose you too. But the next week we had an ultrasound and there you were, waving your little arms, your heart racing.'

'And here I am now,' Beverly would laugh and she would twirl on her toes as her mother laughed with her. Her mother would have been the most wonderful grandmother.

Beverly wipes her eyes. She hates waking up early. She gets maudlin and starts thinking about everyone she's lost. And she has lost so much.

When she was sixteen, she was called out of class to find James in the principal's office, his face pale and his eyes bloodshot. 'Oh, Bev,' he said, grabbing her and holding her tightly. Her parents had been on the way to the Hunter Valley for a wine-tasting weekend when a truck crossed over onto the wrong side of the road. The random, terrible unluckiness of losing both parents has never left Beverly. Sometimes it is a deep sadness that hangs over her, but even after ten years the pain still feels as raw today as it did then. A lot of the time it's an intense anger that two people who were so wonderful were taken in an instant.

She should never have watched the news in the days after her parents died but she had needed to see for herself that it was true because she hadn't been able to absorb the facts. She understood it but it didn't seem real. 'Don't watch the news,' James told her. 'Don't look it up on the internet, just stay off everything for a week or so.' She had nodded as she studied her older brother who was dealing with lawyers and the police, and whose eyes were bloodshot from tears and lack of sleep. She had nodded but she hadn't listened. Instead, when James was asleep, she would creep out of her room and turn the television on at a low volume, watching the news channel for the story that ran for three days after her parents died. Their crumpled red Toyota, their belongings strewn across the highway and the image of the truck driver became imprinted on her mind. Most heartbreaking was her mother's handbag of soft black leather that she and James had given her for her birthday only months before. 'I love it, it's perfect,' she had said to them, her eyes shining with love. She had immediately packed it with all the things she liked to carry and in one shot, as the news camera panned the scene, Beverly noticed a tube of rose-scented hand lotion that her mother carried everywhere with her. It's a smell she always associates with her mother and she thinks that she probably bonded with Marie so quickly because the older woman uses the same scented lotion, rubbing it on her hands after lunch every day in the library.

Beverly's parents were both only children, and as she stood in her long, black, oversized dress – bought for her by James because she wouldn't leave the house before the funeral, Beverly had looked around and seen all their parents' friends but no real family, except for James.

An acute sense of her aloneness, of her vulnerability in the world now that her parents were gone, forced her to squeeze her eyes shut as the horror of a future without her mother and father assaulted her. She wasn't ready to be alone in the world yet, to have to make her own decisions and take care of herself. All through the tea and sympathetic hugs after the funeral she felt herself growing more and more anxious over what would happen to her.

'Will I have to go into foster care?' she asked her brother two days after the funeral, still shell-shocked at how her life had changed. She saw herself having to pack up her room with its sturdy single bed, covered in a bright yellow duvet. She tried to imagine what she would take with her; how much she would be allowed to have. In between bouts of anxiety, she dissolved into tears, her drying cheeks covered in their salty remains.

James grabbed her hand and squeezed it so she would look at him. He always knew when anxiety was clawing at her. 'No, no, absolutely not. Bev, I'm twenty-six. Mum and Dad changed their will so that I'm your legal guardian. They changed it when I turned eighteen. I'm here and you don't have to worry, okay?' Beverly felt her shoulders drop and her stomach cease its endless churning. She wouldn't have to leave behind their little house filled with memories.

'Do you think they knew something, like maybe they had some sort of premonition or something?' she had asked him as the image of the crumpled red Toyota made her shut her eyes, trying to block it all out.

'No, Bev,' he had sighed, rubbing his forehead, forcing his messy, dark-blond hair to stick up at strange angles. 'I think it was just bad luck and a drunk truck driver. They just made a practical decision when I was old enough. And now the house is in both our names and I'll be here for you until you're an adult and you can live alone.'

Beverly had been grateful that they could stay in the house in a nice suburb because her father, Martin, had made sure that the mortgage was paid off. He had been working towards retirement when he died, taking a few days a week off work to 'wind down', as he put it.

Now, Beverly hears the sounds of birds greeting the winter morning and closes her eyes for a moment, feeling her mother's soft touch on her forehead on days when she felt unwell, and seeing her father meticulously packing his truck so he knew everything was clean and in place for the next day's work.

She sits up and gets out of bed, heading for the kitchen and her first cup of coffee. She hasn't managed to push away her thoughts this morning, but instead of letting sadness descend she allows a moment of gratitude that she is still able to live in the home she grew up in and to raise her son here. She takes comfort from the family photos of beach holidays in bright blue Decembers that are everywhere, from the old familiar furniture that needs replacing but holds too many memories of movie nights as a family, and from the smell of turpentine that even a decade later still seems to waft through the house from the spare room where her mother used to paint landscapes.

At sixteen, Beverly had struggled with her grief and James had struggled with suddenly being in charge of a teenage girl. They fought more than they ever had before as they tried to navigate paying bills and cooking and cleaning for themselves.

Beverly's grief led her to stupid choices like alcohol and drugs as James lectured and shouted that she needed to stop 'behaving like an idiot'. There were boys who came and went, happy to have a place to go where there was no adult supervision because James was out a lot, at work or dating. It was the momentary forgetting that Beverly craved. Getting drunk or having sex sometimes allowed her to just be in that moment, not thinking about the past or worried about the future, but right there in that moment. And, in that moment, it didn't hurt quite so much.

'You'll get yourself pregnant and into trouble,' James said. He was struggling every day. He had taken over their father's business, training to be a plumber after school, enjoying working with his hands. Before their parents died, he had been working towards buying another truck and employing people to work for him, but grief made him unreliable. There were some days when he couldn't get out of bed and Beverly would leave his breakfast by the door and find it untouched at lunch. She understood he was struggling. But James fought his way back even though it took months before he was able to start working properly again. Things were getting back on track for him eight months after their parents died. He'd even started dating someone seriously, a young woman who Beverly was determined to dislike, even though she was pretty and seemed to make James happy. Beverly resented James for moving forward with his life, for not needing alcohol and quick sex to take away the pain. She had no idea what her future held and she wonders now, as the garden lightens and the winter sun chases away the night-time shadows, if she had known, could she have done something differently? Would she have done something differently?

Stop this now – time for coffee. Beverly adds milk to her coffee and sets it down so she can wake Riley. In his room he is still curled up, but she can see that he's awake.

'Wakey, wakey, rise and shine, the sun is up and you are down,' she sings.

'How come you say that even when it's raining?' He sits up and looks at his window. 'No rain today – excellent, we can play outside at lunchtime. Maybe I'll get another present today.'

Beverly feels her stomach lurch at this thought. 'Maybe,' she says.

Riley gets out of bed, shedding his pyjamas and donning his school uniform quickly, knowing that he'll be allowed time to game before breakfast if he's dressed in his uniform.

'Yesterday I told Mr Benton that I got a present in the mailbox and he liked my book. He knows how much I like Roblox and in maths class he said that he might start playing it on his computer since so many kids in the class like the game.'

'That's nice,' says Beverly. She hopes again that there is nothing in the mailbox from Ethan this morning; if there is, she needs to call him and tell him to stop. He hasn't responded to her texts.

'Mr Benton said that his father used to send him presents from all over the world when he was travelling around being a salesman.'

'Lucky him,' she answers him. 'Mr Benton sounds like a nice teacher.'

'He's the best,' says Riley, grabbing a brush and running it over his hair, achieving nothing with the kinks but she knows better than to do it for him. Even as a toddler he was very independent. 'I do dis myself,' he always said, and she had to wait patiently while he put his shoes on or zipped up a tracksuit top.

He chatters away through breakfast, telling her about his latest achievements on his game, and only when she is waiting in the car, does she think about Ethan again. When Riley climbs into the car, he is beyond excited. 'I told you, I told you,' he crows.

Beverly sighs and picks up her phone, composing a text. *Look, you have to stop leaving gifts for Riley. It's not fair on him. Please just give me some space.*

'Can I open it?' asks Riley. The present is, once again, wrapped in blue paper with silver stars. It's a fairly big box this time.

'How did that fit in the mailbox?' Beverly asks.

'It was on the ground, didn't you see it?' says Riley, running his hands over the paper.

'Isn't the paper wet?' she asks, knowing that the grass underneath the mailbox would have been damp from the overnight cold.

'A bit, not much, can I open it?'

She can hear he's getting frustrated, but she puts out her hand and he gives it to her with a dramatic sigh. Once again there is the same card with the same message. The paper is only slightly damp which means that the present was left only recently. Beverly feels a shiver run through her body. She heard a noise this morning. Maybe that was Ethan dropping off the gift. She hates the idea that he's coming to their house.

'Here you go,' she says, handing Riley the box and watching as he opens it.

'Way cool,' he says when he sees what it is. 'Look, Mum,' he says, holding the box up. 'It's so I can build a robot – and you know what the best thing is?'

She waits, watching his green eyes dance with joy. 'Mr Benton is teaching us about robots at school in science. Isn't that the best thing ever?'

'Yes,' she says, feeling unease run through her. 'It's the best thing.'

Instead of just dropping Riley off, Beverly parks and gets out of the car when they arrive at school.

'What's happening?' he asks, knowing that she never does this. She always drops him in the kiss-and-go area.

'I thought I would come and meet Mr Benton since he's so nice,' she says, keeping her tone light.

'Oh, you'll love him,' says Riley and he grabs her hand and pulls her to the school front gate. She has to run a little to keep up with him, but she can't help smiling at his excitement at her meeting his teacher. Soon, probably sooner than she would like, he will no longer want to hold her hand, so she relishes the feeling of his cold fingers, slightly calloused from all the tree climbing, in hers.

As they enter the school he looks around. 'He's not here,' he says, his face falling. 'Maybe he's running late?'

Beverly looks at her watch. 'I can't really wait, maybe tomorrow,' she says to him, even though she would have liked to speak to the teacher, just to introduce herself. He and Riley do seem to be having some odd conversations.

'Okay, bye, Mum,' Riley says as he spots Benji and runs to tell him about his latest present. He has the robot kit in his backpack because he is sure that Mr Benton will want to see it.

She walks back to her car quickly, aware that she's running late but as she walks, she calls Ethan's phone and gets his voicemail. 'Ethan, I know you want to talk and we will, but I need you to stop leaving gifts for Riley. It's not fair on him.'

She hangs up and gets into the car. As she pulls out, she almost hits another car driving past. The driver hoots at her and she slams on her brakes, her heart racing and her mouth dry. She's not concentrating. She looks up to apologise to the other driver, but he drives away and all she sees is a glimpse of brown hair and an arm in a striped shirt. She leaves her parking spot carefully and slowly, making sure to look for children in the road.

Beverly hopes Riley's teacher lets him build the robot in class. It's not something she would be very good at and the toy looks quite complicated. She would probably need more technical ability to actually construct it. She wonders if Sam would be able to help Riley. He was, she remembers, an engineer. She smiles as she remembers this, content that she will be able to get Riley some help if the teacher says the toy is not for school. As she pulls into her designated parking spot outside the library, she has a flashback to James and her father working on a remote-control car together, their heads bent over small parts, their soft voices discussing where bits might go. A boy needs a father, but she cannot risk what they have by bringing a man into her life. She simply cannot.

She takes a deep breath, an overwhelming sadness bringing tears to her eyes. The loss of her parents was a horrible, random accident. The loss of James was something else altogether.

CHAPTER TEN

Riley

'What do you think?' Mr Benton asks Riley as they study the robot.

'I think it's amazing,' says Benji. Mr Benton has agreed to help the boys build the kit over lunch. Some of the other boys and girls were watching them for a while but most of them got bored when Mr Benton said that since it was Riley's gift, he should be the one building it. Riley had wanted Benji involved but no one else. Only he and Benji knew that the present was probably from his dad the spy.

'I bet… I bet, right,' said Benji as they were laying all the parts out on a desk, 'that once it's done, you'll turn it on and maybe it will make you follow it and then it will take you straight to your dad.'

'Yeah,' agreed Riley, and he had felt like he did the night before his birthday or Christmas, just filled up with excitement. He wanted to jump up and down and clap his hands, but he didn't do that because he wasn't a baby anymore and Mr Benton was watching him.

'I think we should start with the instructions,' Mr Benton said. 'And I don't think this robot can lead you to your dad, Riley.' He said it softly but Riley trusted Mr Benton and just like that, he felt sad.

'I bet it can,' Benji whispered into Riley's ear, but he whispered it so loudly that Mr Benton heard.

'You boys,' said Mr Benton laughing. They had worked quietly for a few minutes. 'I bet your mum could get you a book on robots from her library,' said Mr Benton.

'Maybe, or I could get one from the school library. Her library is really small and it's filled with old people. I don't think old people like robots. Ethan loved robots.'

'Who's Ethan?' asked Mr Benton.

'He was Riley's mum's boyfriend but now they're like broken up and Riley is sad 'cause he was nice,' Benji said, picking up a bolt and attempting to twirl it on his finger.

'Oh right, yes, you told me about that, but you didn't tell me his name,' said Mr Benton. 'Maybe she'll find a new boyfriend.'

'Maybe,' said Riley.

'You could be her boyfriend, Mr Benton,' said Benji, 'unless you already have a girlfriend.'

'No,' said Mr Benton, 'I don't… I used to but—'

'Do you have kids?' asked Benji, even though Riley could see that Mr Benton didn't want to talk about stuff like that. Some teachers didn't mind sharing everything with the kids they taught. Mrs Emmerson, who taught him and Benji last year, had told them everything that happened in her life, including when she got a new puppy and the best day ever was when she brought the puppy into school so they could all see him. He was cute but he had sharp little teeth.

'I have a son,' said Mr Benton quietly, 'but I haven't spent time with him in a long time. I'm hoping to change that.' It didn't sound like he was talking to them, more like he was talking to himself as he tightened the small screws at the bottom of the robot.

'How old—' began Benji who never knew when to stop asking questions.

'Let's not discuss it anymore.' Mr Benton stopped talking and then they only discussed the robot until it was done.

'Put it on the floor and make it move to the door,' says Mr Benton.

Riley picks up the robot and puts it down on the ground. He moves the switches up and down on the remote control, turning the robot one way and then another, and then it heads straight for Mr Benton, bumping into his foot.

'You'll get the hang of it,' says Mr Benton and Benji starts laughing, making Riley's ears get hot.

'Maybe Mr Benton is your father,' says Benji and then they all laugh because Mr Benton is their teacher and Riley's father is a spy.

CHAPTER ELEVEN

She nearly caught me this morning. I don't know how she heard me, but I saw the lights go on all over the house and felt my heart in my throat. I crouched down behind her car and waited until the lights went off again. I knew he'd just love the present. I went into the store yesterday late in the afternoon, knowing exactly what I wanted to get him. There was only one left on the shelf and as I reached for it, a woman reached for it as well.

'Oh,' she said, smiling and flustered, 'it's for my son's birthday – do you mind?'

I sighed quietly and perhaps she thought she was getting the robot kit because she grabbed it, but I wasn't giving in that easily. I said, 'Actually, it's for my son's birthday as well. I don't get to see him much because of the divorce and he really likes robots. It's been such a hard time for him.'

She immediately let go of the toy. People don't expect to hear your sad life story in the toy aisle of Kmart and I watched her face colour as she struggled for something comforting to say.

'Gosh, thank you,' I said, giving her a smile, and she nodded her head and smiled back, almost running to get away from me. I'm sure she thought I was some weirdo but I don't care about that. I didn't want to get him anything else. The kit wasn't too expensive but tomorrow he will get the most expensive present of all and then… then everything will fall into place.

I know what I'm doing with the presents. When I explain who I am, when I tell him the truth, I will start with the fact that I gave him the gifts. Over the past year, since I found out the truth, I have been looking at 'toys for eight-year-old boys' on the web. He was seven when I found him, but I knew he would be older when I met him. Things have changed since I was a child. They even teach maths differently now, which is weird, but you can get used to it pretty quickly. I have done a lot of research on children and what they need and want. I even have some menus planned for when I start giving him lunch and dinner. I think good nutrition is important for children, although a treat is always permitted.

I wrapped the gift carefully in my basement room, thrilled with how happy he would be to get it. When I crept out of Sam's house this morning, Scotty didn't even lift his little head to look at me. He is used to my comings and goings now.

She doesn't know that I watch her at night, that I come out here in the cold and the dark just to look at her. She's very pretty. I think she looks better without make-up on. I like to see her moving around the kitchen as she cleans up, occasionally saying something to him and then smiling, or looking deep in thought. Sometimes she simply stands still and closes her eyes and I can see how tired she is then. I wonder what she's thinking about, what memories are there, what thoughts. Raising a child is difficult. Raising a child that you have no right to be raising must be even harder and I imagine she has a lot of sleepless nights.

I can't remember the last time I slept well. After my parents told me to leave, I had to find a way to make money. I didn't have a degree or any qualifications, so all I could get were menial jobs. The jobs got better after I learned how easy it was to fake a résumé and a university degree. But the jobs, both good and bad, were never what drove me. I was missing something in my life, something that I should have experienced as a child but never did. I missed the sense of being home, not just in a house but the feeling of home.

All I ever wanted was a real family, a family where I was in charge and where I was loved and respected. I had an image that I went back to again and again when I was worried about late rent and an empty grocery cupboard. It was the image of a house, a lot like the one I had grown up in, with a stone wall in the front, covered in jasmine in the spring. The house I grew up in had three bedrooms and two bathrooms and a kitchen with timber cupboards and a stone countertop. My mother loved the kitchen, insisting on the best of everything when it was redone when I was fifteen and my sister was fourteen. We had to be really careful in there after that. The stone stained easily and my mother was nearly hysterical about keeping it clean. I was always careful to pour myself juice in the sink, terrified of what would happen if I spilled something. But in the house in my mind the countertop never stains and the mess can always be cleaned away. In the kitchen in my mind there is a round table with a flowered tablecloth and a happy child eating his breakfast. And when he looks at me, I can see that he loves me and he feels safe with me. That's all I want; all I have ever wanted. It would have been nice to be a real little family with a mother and father and two children, but it's too late for that now. Now I will just have to be a single parent. But being a single parent is better than not being a parent at all.

I am lying on my bed imagining every detail of my dream home, how the flowers will be planted in rows and there will be a neat brick pathway to the front door. I will become friendly with the neighbours and my son will talk about how hard I work to take care of him. 'It's just the two of us,' he will tell people and they will smile and nod and perhaps try to set me up on dates.

There is a small niggle inside me, a feeling that what I'm about to do is wrong and I have to keep pushing it away. I'm not asking for much. I've never asked for much. I shouldn't have had to work this hard to get what I want.

I hear Sam call Scotty for bed. I didn't know how long I would be here or how smoothly it would go, but so far everything has gone according to plan. Tomorrow I will give him the most expensive gift. Tomorrow will change everything and then the next step will be easy.

CHAPTER TWELVE

Beverly

Thursday

Before she gets Riley up, Beverly lets herself out of the house quietly, pulling her robe around her neck as the cold air hits her skin.

She has sent Ethan three text messages and called him four times and he hasn't responded to her at all. He's angry with her, she understands that, but not responding is rude.

Beverly breathes out and watches her breath condense in the air. The mornings are getting colder and colder, and she reminds herself to make sure that the jacket she bought Riley last year still fits. She bought it at least two sizes too big but he seems to get taller every day. She never knew it was possible to see someone grow overnight until Riley. Even when he was a baby, she would put him to bed some nights and in the morning a onesie that fitted him the night before had grown too tight for his long body.

She opens the top of the mailbox and curses when she sees that there is indeed a gift. It's a rectangle shape, and quite heavy. This really has gone on for long enough. She looks at the note which is exactly the same as all the other ones. Perhaps she should go and see Ethan at work. If he's being this difficult, she might have to. She tucks the present under her arm and turns around.

'What are you doing?'

Beverly yelps in fright and drops the present on the ground. 'Riley,' she yells, 'what are you doing? Why are you sneaking up on me?'

He looks down at the gift on the ground. 'You were going to hide that from me, weren't you?' he asks, a hint of menace in his voice. He puts his hands on his hips, the same way she does when she's about to give him a lecture about poor behaviour.

Beverly wants to tell him to watch his tone, but he's caught her red-handed and she cannot think how to explain why she was going to hide the gift. He's only eight. He wouldn't understand.

'Now listen, Riley,' she begins, and then she notices that he has come outside in his pyjamas without slippers. It's really cold. 'Let's go inside,' she says and leans down to get the gift but he's quicker than she is. He grabs it and darts back into the house, his hands tearing at the paper as he goes.

She stalks back into the kitchen behind him, her hands already reaching out for whatever it is when he stops ripping the paper and says, 'Whoa – look at this!' His eyes are saucers in his face, disbelief in his voice.

It's a Nintendo Switch, a coveted toy at Riley's school. She knows that it's at least four hundred dollars. He opens the box and pulls out the device, dropping the box on the floor. He touches the switch to turn it on and the screen lights up. It's already charged and ready to go. She bites her lip while he starts navigating the device, his movements sure. Benji's older brother has one and she knows that Riley and Benji have been allowed to play on it if Jeremy is in a good mood.

'It's got games loaded on as well. This is just the best thing ever,' he says, looking at her, and she can read the hope on his face. He sits down at the table, murmuring, 'whoa' and 'cool' each time he clicks on to a new screen.

'I'm sorry, you can't keep that,' she whispers, hating that she has to disappoint him like this, but it's too expensive, there's too much meaning attached to it. She had discussed buying him this present with Ethan and she knew that she would never be able to afford it for his birthday in August, but she was hoping that if she cut back on takeaway lunches from twice to once a week and brought her own coffee in to work, she would be able to give it to him for Christmas. There were a few children in his year who had the games console and it was something they all talked about. It's at the top of Riley's list of dream presents.

His face falls and she can see him gritting his teeth as he navigates through screens on the device. 'It's mine,' he says, his voice hard with emotion. 'It's a present for me and you can't take it away from me. That's like stealing.' The tips of his ears turn red which happens when he gets angry or embarrassed.

She steps forward and touches the game, watches as he holds on tightly so she has to pull to get it away from him. 'Let go, Riley. You cannot keep this. It's too expensive and we don't even know who to thank for it.'

Riley refuses to let go, his eyes scrunching with anger, baring his teeth at her. 'It's mine, mine, mine,' he repeats, his voice becoming a growl. 'You didn't give it to me and you can't take it away.'

'I'm your mother and I say it has to go back. You cannot keep this.' She grunts with the effort of trying to get it away from him. They tussle like this for another few moments and then Riley abruptly lets go of the Switch and she falls backwards, trying to stop herself but failing as she bashes into the sharp edge of the wall behind her. 'Ow,' she cries and drops the console.

She lifts her hand to her head, feeling for tenderness, unable to conceal her tears. *How could you do this to me, Ethan? How could you be so cruel?*

Riley stands up from the table, his face ashen with shock at her tears and at having caused her to hurt herself. 'Mum… Mum… Mum, I'm sorry, I'm sorry,' he says, tears appearing on his face.

Beverly closes her eyes and takes a deep breath. She clenches her fists and counts to ten to calm herself. He's sorry, she knows that. She opens her eyes and sniffs, wiping her face and holding out her arms for him to step into, which he does, wrapping his arms around her waist and burying his head in the blue fluff of the gown, his crying loud and heartbreaking.

'It's okay, it's okay,' Beverly soothes, wishing that there was someone to soothe her and then hating herself because she did have someone and she sent him away. As angry as she is at Ethan, she cannot hate him because he is only trying to get her to talk to him. Still, there are better ways than anonymous gifts.

Once they have dried their tears, she picks up the device and shoves it at the top of one of the kitchen cupboards.

'When I've figured out who it's from, we'll discuss it, okay?' she says. She doesn't want to tell Riley that it's from Ethan. It will only hurt more that he is no longer in their lives. 'Now go and get dressed please. We're going to be late for school.'

Riley is subdued through breakfast and she doesn't have the energy to try and talk him into being cheerful. He really wanted the games console and she doesn't know if she will be able to keep it from him. She will just have to get hold of Ethan and tell him he has to explain to Riley that they've broken up. Maybe she can convince Ethan to say the gifts were a kind of goodbye. If he'll tell Riley that then she'll let him keep it. She relaxes at this thought. It will be a good way for everything to end and Riley can always think of Ethan fondly. That way, she won't resent him so much for having bought a toy for her son that he knows she was saving up for. All the gifts were goodbye gifts. She's happy with that idea.

They drive to school in silence and she stops in the kiss-and-go section outside the gates. 'Have a good day,' she says quietly.

'I bet if I had a dad, he would have let me keep it,' says Riley and she understands that he has been ruminating on this thought all the way to school. She has no idea what to say to him.

'We'll discuss it later,' she says shortly.

He opens the car door and heaves his backpack out with him, 'Mr Benton said he thinks a Nintendo Switch is the best fun. I bet he would have let me keep it as well.'

I bet everyone you know is nicer than I am. 'See you later,' she says and he slams the car door, hard. He is angry with her but she's angry with him as well. She puts her hand up to touch the back of her head, feeling the growing lump there. Behind her a car hoots and she pulls off and drives to work, only remembering once she's there that she had meant to go and meet Riley's new teacher. Her cheeks flush as she imagines Riley telling him that his mean mother wouldn't let him keep the gift. She hates the idea that he may be saying things about her to anyone in authority. The worry that someone somewhere will decide he is not meant to be with her is always there. Mothers who are considered unfit have their children taken away all the time. She's finding Riley's constant mentioning of the new teacher strange, and she still has no real information on him. It would probably make sense to call the school and have a chat with someone about who he is and where he taught before, but she doesn't have the energy for that right now. Mentally, Beverly puts it on her list of things to do tomorrow.

As Beverly walks into work, she calls Ethan again; it goes through to his voicemail. 'Look, Ethan, I really need to talk to you about these gifts. Giving Riley a Switch without consulting me is unacceptable and you need to know I haven't let him have it. But I'm willing to give it to him as long as you can assure me that it's over now. I'll get him to call and thank you, but we need to talk first. Please call me.'

She will give him another day or two to respond and then she will turn up at his office and confront him. She's never visited him at the company where he works in the city, so she will need time off from the library. But Marie will understand – she was upset for Beverly over the break-up.

'But why?' Marie had said. 'He was so lovely with Riley and whenever you talked on the phone, I could always hear you laughing. You seemed to get on so well.'

'It just wasn't right,' Beverly told the older woman, because what else was she going to say?

As she walks into work Beverly's muscles relax a little, even as she can feel her stomach protesting against her morning coffee. She breathes in the smell of old books and the dust that returns no matter how much they clean, and she is comforted by the warmth from the air conditioner. Smiling at the cheery children's corner, decorated with prints from children's books and filled with colourful beanbags, she is grateful to be at work. She has always felt safe here; safe and welcomed.

Behind the front counter where their computers and the machines for checking out books stand, is a small office that Beverly and Marie retreat to when no one is in the library. She takes a quick look around, making sure no one is there, and then ducks into the office to put her bag down.

Marie is reading the newspaper, standing over her desk with her head in her hands, her glasses on the end of her nose.

'You won't believe what Ethan left for Riley today,' Beverly says and explains about the Switch when Marie looks up at her.

'That's a really expensive gift,' says Marie. 'You're right. It's unacceptable. It's so strange that he's doing this. But maybe he's working up to some grand gesture to you, like… riding into the library on a white horse and proposing.'

Beverly laughs despite her concern. 'Maybe you can really only see the romantic side of this but I'm getting a little freaked out by it. I've asked him to leave us alone and he should have done that. I can only imagine how much worse it's going to get if this is not the end. I mean, imagine if I have to go to the police to get him to stop sending things to my son. It's getting downright weird.'

Marie nods her head. 'You're right, I was just trying to make you smile. It's not right. If you need me to come with you to see him and make sure he understands I will do that.'

'I might just ask you to,' says Beverly. She lifts up the kettle that sits on a small table, checking that it is full before switching it on to make some mint herbal tea for herself, hoping it will settle her churning stomach. She hunts through her bag for a muesli bar, knowing that she needs to eat or she'll start to feel nauseous. As she chews on a bite, savouring the dark chocolate and nuts, she glances down at the newspaper.

'Anything interesting?' she asks as she swallows because she doesn't want Marie to think she's angry at her. Marie refuses to read the news on the internet, preferring to get it the old-fashioned way.

'The usual,' says Marie as she gets a packet of chocolate biscuits from her desk drawer, pulling out one to eat with her own cup of tea. 'The world is a sad, sad place and I'm happy that I get to be here, surrounded by books and cocooned away from it all. There was an interesting article about primary school teachers not being qualified to teach. Apparently, the government schools are not checking résumés thoroughly enough.'

'Teaching is such a difficult job,' says Beverly. 'I can't imagine anyone wanting to walk into a classroom without the proper qualifications.'

Riley's new teacher crosses her mind and she takes a quick look at her computer, logging on to the website for Riley's school and looking at 'This Week's News':

Mrs Patricia Randall is recovering well after her operation to set a broken arm and we are delighted to welcome Mr Alexander Benton as a substitute teacher from Melbourne to take care of her lovely year three class.

Beverly types Alexander Benton into Google but even though hundreds of results come up, no 'Alexander Benton, teacher' is listed. She starts going through Facebook profiles but then hears someone saying 'Excuse me,' at the front desk. She closes Google, reminding herself to take another look later tonight as she goes out to help a library patron.

Mr Benton is obviously a qualified teacher. Riley's school principal would have made sure of that.

CHAPTER THIRTEEN
Riley

'Maybe you could creep out of bed at night and play it. She doesn't need to know,' says Benji. They are sitting on top of the monkey bars together, legs swinging as they watch the year four boys and girls playing a game of tag. They've had their turn on the handball court, but Riley wasn't all that interested in playing. He can't stop thinking about the Switch, which he saw has the latest Mario Kart game on it. It's the best present he's ever gotten.

'I bet my dad would be really angry with her if he knew that she won't let me play with it,' he says.

'Yeah,' agrees Benji and he picks his nose and flicks it onto the ground.

'Gross,' laughs Riley and Benji shrugs.

'And maybe I could have a sleepover at yours on Saturday night and then we could play together.'

'Yeah,' agrees Riley, nodding enthusiastically.

'Lunch is nearly over, boys, maybe it's time to climb down,' says Mr Benton, looking up at the two of them from under the monkey bars.

'Mr Benton, guess what?' says Benji.

'What?'

'Riley got another anon… anon… present from someone and it was a Switch, but his mum was mean and said he couldn't have it and now… we don't know what to do because it was for him and she should let him play with it.'

'Well,' says Mr Benton, looking down at his black sneakers, the same sneakers he wears every day, 'I guess she must have her reasons.'

'Like what?' asks Riley, scratching his chin.

'Maybe she doesn't like the person who gave it to you or maybe she thinks it's too expensive or maybe she doesn't like video games.'

'I bet if she could talk to the person who gave it to me, she would let me play with it.'

'Maybe she already has already talked to him,' says Mr Benton.

'Yeah, course she has, Riley,' says Benji. 'It's your dad. She must have talked to your dad. They had to do like… sex stuff to make a baby.'

Mr Benton laughs. 'Come on, you two, time to come down.'

'My mum came to meet you yesterday, Mr Benton, but you were late,' says Riley as he climbs down the ladder to get to the ground.

'I was late,' the teacher agrees. 'I was up all night watching… television and I overslept. I can meet your mum at our parent–teacher appointment next term.'

'But won't Mrs Randall be back? Her arm will be better unless she's dead,' says Benji, looking up at his teacher who has shiny green eyes.

'I don't think she's dead and don't worry, I'll meet your mum, Riley. I will definitely meet her.'

CHAPTER FOURTEEN

I am out in Sam's garden, at the back behind the tall hedge. The cold wind feels rough against my cheeks but the sky is a glaringly bright winter blue. I positioned myself here twenty minutes ago, knowing that he will be outside and climbing up this tree very soon.

The time has come to introduce myself to him; well, not introduce, rather explain who I am. It's not like I'm a stranger. Before this week, I hadn't seen him for a long time but I'm definitely not a stranger.

I have moments when I am afraid of how difficult it's going to be to convince him that he should be with me and only me. Children like routine and he won't want to leave his home, his bedroom, his mother. I know that.

But I'm sure that if I can get him to listen to me, to allow me to tell him the truth about who he is and who he should be with, he'll be happy to be with me. I don't want to think about what will happen if he's not.

In my head, I imagine a joyful reunion as soon as he understands and knows the truth. In my head he only wants to be with me and she realises that she has no choice but to let him go.

But there is a chance that it will not go the way I want it to go. There's a chance that he will question the truth, that he won't believe me when I tell him what happened. And if that happens then I know what I will have to do. If there is a choice to be made between me and Beverly, then there needs to be no choice at all. I will need to narrow down the choices from two to one. My hands shake and I start to sweat when I imagine causing harm to another person. It won't be the first time. Last time I let anger overwhelm me and I won't make the same mistake this time. I shake my head, banishing memories of a face, mouth open, huge staring eyes, absolute terror in the gaze.

I wanted it to happen, but I hadn't planned it.

This time, I have a plan. This time, I will stay focused.

CHAPTER FIFTEEN
Beverly

When Beverly arrives to pick Riley up from school, he doesn't run to her the way he usually does. Instead, he walks past her and out the school gates towards where he knows she usually parks the car. Another mother throws her a rueful glance and she smiles and shrugs her shoulders in the silent communication of all mothers whose children are having a bad day.

She has tried calling Ethan so many times today that she's beginning to feel like she is his stalker.

'Well,' Marie had said when they talked about the gifts again over lunch, 'you would think this might be last the last one. I mean, how much more expensive can the gifts become? Perhaps it was just his way of saying goodbye and this will be the end of it.'

'I hope that's right,' Beverly said, pleased that Marie agreed with her thinking. 'But I feel like I need to speak to him, just clear the air, and then maybe I can make Riley send a thank you email and that will be the last of it. All I need is for him to return my calls.'

Marie had frowned as she bit into her chicken and lettuce sandwich. 'It's odd that he hasn't answered any calls or texts, don't you think? Is it like him to be so,' she waved a hand in the air, 'so... I don't know... maddening?'

'It's definitely driving me mad,' Beverly replied, struggling to swallow the bite of sushi in her mouth as she remembered Ethan turning up at work in February on Valentine's Day with a picnic basket. He had said, 'I know you only have an hour's break and that you don't really leave the library, but I've cleared it with Marie and we can sit in the park across the road and have a quick lunch.' He had packed a beautiful picnic of cheese and French bread, delicate macarons flavoured with tiramisu cream and a half bottle of wine so they could have one glass each before returning to work.

'You're a good man,' she told him as they sat with their backs against a large tree, enjoying the slight breeze and the shade.

'You're a wonderful woman,' he had said.

Beverly doesn't know how Ethan could be doing something that would hurt her and Riley.

'Did you meet Riley's new teacher?' Marie asked, startling Beverly from her thoughts.

'Not yet,' she said. 'But I will tomorrow morning, I hope, when things are a little calmer. I tried looking him up online but there's nothing about him on the internet. He's from Melbourne.'

'It's freezing there now,' Marie said.

All hopes Beverly had of Riley getting over the games console disappear as he climbs into the car and buckles his seat belt, a scowl on his face. He stares out of the window, refusing to even look at her.

'Look,' she says, determined to tackle the problem before he spends his whole afternoon sulking, 'I think I know who the gifts are from and when I speak to the person, I will explain that the Nintendo was too expensive but if they say that they want you to have it – then you can have it.' She glances at Riley's face in the rear-view mirror.

He has his arms crossed but he relaxes. 'Who is the person?' He looks at the mirror as well, meeting her gaze.

'I'm not sure.'

'I think… and Benji thinks, that it's from my dad,' he says softly.

Beverly takes a deep breath, feels her shoulders tense. 'Riley, your dad isn't alive anymore. I know that's a hard thing to have to deal with. I know because my dad, your grandpa, isn't alive anymore either and it's okay to feel sad about it. I feel sad about it all the time. But I know, for sure, that the gifts are not coming from your father.' She looks back at him but he is staring out of the window. He's listening but she knows that he doesn't believe her.

'How did he die?' Riley asks. It's not a question he's ever asked before.

'In a car accident,' she says, because this is the easiest thing to tell him.

'What, like my grandmother and grandfather? Were they together?'

Beverly's cheeks flush, her palms feel clammy on the steering wheel. 'No, no. It was um… another car accident. It was late at night and he was coming home from work and—'

'What was his work?' Riley asks and Beverly takes a hand off the steering wheel to massage her neck where tension is causing a shooting pain into her head.

'He was a plumber.'

'Just like your dad,' laughs Riley. 'Did your dad know him?'

'Yes,' she says, tears burning her eyes, 'he did know him. He worked for your grandfather before…' She stops talking because now the pain is lodged in her heart as well and she can't give into it. She needs to focus, to explain to her little boy that his father is not the one sending him presents, but she doesn't know if he will believe her. 'I promise you, Riley, that he's not alive anymore.'

As she says the words, Beverly realises that she doesn't fully believe them herself. She doesn't want to; she imagines a scenario in which he turns up at her door and confesses to not being dead, but to being alive and just… just what?

She rubs her head, trying to rub away the pain, and swipes her cheeks so he doesn't see her tears. 'I think,' she says, knowing that she is not ready to tell him, but needing to put this idea of his father being alive to rest, 'that the gifts may be from Ethan.'

Riley is quiet and she knows this is because she has given him an explanation that he knows is true.

'Maybe... maybe he wanted to be my dad,' says Riley, scratching his chin.

Beverly wishes she could pull over and take him in her arms as she hears the touch of heartbreak in his voice, but she keeps driving instead, as ways to explain things and words to use that might comfort him circle in her head.

At a traffic light she turns and looks at her son. 'Listen, baby, I know that what happened between me and Ethan is hard for you, but there are some things, some things that I will explain when you're older about people and relationships.' The car behind her taps politely on their hooter and she turns around again and drives as she chews on her lip.

She keeps waiting for him to say something else. When he speaks, it's obvious he's crying. 'I'm never gonna have a dad, I mean an alive dad, am I?'

Beverly's eyes spill over as she contemplates her own cruelty towards the one human being she loves most in the world. If he knew the truth, if everyone knew the truth, then she wouldn't be piling one lie on top of another. 'I don't know, baby. I wish I could tell you, but you need to know that I love you more than anything in the whole world and I will be there for you forever.'

She doesn't know what else she could say to him, how else to explain it to him. Once he gets to eighteen and he can no longer be taken from her, she will tell him the truth. Until then she needs to maintain the status quo.

When they arrive home, Riley looks hopefully at the cupboard where she's put the Switch, but he doesn't say anything.

'The moment I speak to Ethan and make sure that you can write him a thank you email, you can have it, I promise you,' she says.

'Have you called him or like texted or something?' he asks, suspicious that she is just fobbing him off.

'Absolutely. He's probably busy with work and will get back to me tonight. You just need to give me until then, okay?' She doesn't believe the words herself, but Riley doesn't need to know that.

She is aware as she speaks that she is giving in; little by little she is moving towards simply giving him the Switch, even if she doesn't hear from Ethan.

'Okay,' he says and he drops his school bag in the kitchen and gets himself a glass from the cupboard, standing on tiptoes to do so.

'Do you have homework?'

'Nah,' he says, filling the glass and splashing his shirt in the process. 'Mr Benton went home early and we had a substitute so we just did art. I drew my new Switch and Benji said that it looks awesome. Can I get apple and peanut butter for snack?'

'Sure,' she says, and busies herself cutting up Riley's apple and putting a spoonful of peanut butter next to it. 'Why did Mr Benton go home?'

'I don't know but Benji said...' He goes quiet in the kitchen and all she can hear is the crunch of the apple in his mouth.

'Benji said what?' she asks as she takes a pot out to make spaghetti.

'Benji said that he should be your new boyfriend. He's got brown hair like I do and if you saw him and me together, he could be my... new dad.'

Beverly sighs. 'Oh, Riley, sweetheart, that's very nice of Benji to find me a boyfriend but I don't need one, really, I just need you.'

'Yeah, I told him that.' He shrugs and then stands up. 'I'm gonna go to the garden now. Call me if you speak to Ethan. If you let me play on the Switch tonight, I promise, promise that I'll be extra good this weekend and let you have a long sleep in on Saturday.'

'Promise, promise?' Beverly asks, smiling as she fills the pot with water for pasta and hunts out a smaller one to make the sauce.

'Yeah,' he says and he darts out of the kitchen to his room to change, and before she's even begun chopping onions, he whizzes past her into the pantry for his bag of chips. He has his iPad and she's pleased to see that he's wearing a jumper with his short pants. She opens her mouth to tell him he needs long pants because of the chill in the air, but he's already out the door and running towards the tree before she can ever form the sentence.

'Promise, promise,' she murmurs to herself as she chops onions, remembering her parents telling her and James that they would take them camping the following weekend or that they could have cake for dessert or that they were allowed to watch television until late on the weekend. 'Promise, promise?' James always asked, needing to make sure whatever treat he was waiting for would happen. 'Promise, promise,' her mother always said. 'Yay!' she and James would respond. A 'promise, promise' meant there was no way for her parents to back out or change their minds. The last time she heard those words from James comes back to her and she can almost see him standing in front of her, his dark-blond hair too long and curling at the collar, his forehead furrowed with worry, shadows under his eyes.

'I'll help you,' she had said to him. 'I promise.'

'Promise, promise?' he asked and she had nodded and given him a hug.

'Promise, promise, big brother.'

Her hands keep moving, chopping the onions into smaller and smaller pieces, as she allows her tears to fall, knowing that she can explain them away to her son because chopping onions makes everyone cry.

CHAPTER SIXTEEN
Riley

Riley rubs his knee where he has scraped it climbing up the tree. He should have put on long pants but it's not that sore.

His mum is going to give him the Switch and that's all he can think about. *Maybe.* Maybe she's going to give him the Switch if Ethan says he can have it. He'll write him a good email and say thanks for it.

He looks towards the kitchen where his mum has already switched the light on so she can cook, and he thinks about Ethan. He didn't like him at first because he tried really hard to be Riley's friend and Riley has Benji for that and some other kids at school. What he really wanted, what he dreams about having, is a dad. Benji and his dad go on camping weekends with Benji's brothers; they catch fish and make fires and roast marshmallows. Benji always says Riley can come with him, but it feels like it's something a dad and his kids should do, not a dad and his kids' friends. His mum hates camping because she's afraid of snakes and spiders and she doesn't like sleeping outside.

At first, when Ethan started coming over, Riley got kind of angry, but after a few weeks he sort of liked him a lot. It was weird to wake up one day and have his mum just say that they weren't going to see him anymore. He misses Ethan. He was a good guy and he probably would have been a good dad and Ethan loved camping. Riley goes back to his game, making some moves so he doesn't think about stuff that bothers him. Excitement over the Switch rises up inside him. His very own Switch. It's the best thing ever and Benji will be so happy to know he is allowed to keep it.

Maybe Benji can sleep over on Friday night and they can play all night. He looks up from his game over to the kitchen window where he sometimes sees his mum looking at him. She's not there now. He opens his packet of chips and crunches three into his mouth so that he can play Roblox while he chews. There's spaghetti for dinner tonight and he loves spaghetti, and he's going to get to play with the Switch. Today is turning into the best day ever, except for the fact that Mr Benton is not going to be their teacher anymore. Riley doesn't know why that is, but this afternoon, when art was supposed to be finished, their principal Miss Abelson came to tell them that tomorrow they would have a new teacher.

'Again?' said Benji. 'Why?'

'Mr Benton had a family emergency,' Miss Abelson told them, but she didn't say what it was, just that he had to leave and they were going to do art for the rest of the day. Now it means that his mum won't even get to meet him and that makes Riley a little sad. He forgot to tell his mum about Mr Benton leaving because he was still mad about the Switch, but he'll tell her when he goes inside for dinner. He wishes Mr Benton would have stayed because then he could have told him about Ethan giving him the Switch and his mum letting him play on it. The wind rushes around the garden and blows the dead leaves around and Riley shivers. He looks up and looks around. It's very quiet except for some lawnmower going somewhere but he feels a bit weird, his skin shivery and strange, like someone's watching him. He laughs because he's high up in the tree and he's the one watching people. Crunching up the last of his chips and dropping the packet on the ground to pick up later, he goes back to his game.

CHAPTER SEVENTEEN

I take a deep breath. *Here we go*, I think. I make my way out of the hedge and into the back garden, making sure to walk slowly and carefully so that I don't make any noise. I don't want him to see me just yet. I want to be in position, just standing casually without any sort of apparent threat. Fortunately, there is a lawnmower going that drowns out the sound of me moving through the garden. There is always a lawnmower going somewhere in this suburb.

I stand behind the rotting garden shed, as I have done for the last few days, and watch him for a few moments. His eyes are scrunched up with the effort of seeing the screen on his iPad in the low afternoon sun, his mouth moving quickly as he eats. He's not playing on the Switch and while this makes my heart sink a little, it actually suits me. He will be more malleable. I'm willing to bet he begged and pleaded to be allowed to play on it when he got home from school. I picture the two of them having a big argument and him storming off to his tree. I can use that to my advantage.

I take a deep breath and step out from behind the shed, moving towards the back fence where the fallen tree sits. There is grass and moss growing over it, I see as I get close to it, so presumably it's been here for a long time and neither Sam nor Beverly has made a move to do anything about it.

He still hasn't seen me, so fierce is his concentration on the game.

I stand right next to the fallen tree. 'Hello,' I call. He doesn't respond, his fingers dancing across the screen. I clear my throat.

'Hello,' I call loudly.

A shiver of worry makes me clench my fists. *What if she is watching right now?* She could be standing at the kitchen window looking right at me. I can imagine her panic at seeing me here in this garden, talking to him. Would she open the door and call out to me if she saw me? Would she come running across the garden, panic making her stumble and trip? Would she understand what I have planned? I don't know how quickly she could move, or if he would understand why she was so worried, and I have to admit that the idea of her fear is a delicious warmth inside me. She should be afraid. She did a terrible thing and now she's going to pay for it by having her world upended. It's all she deserves.

I'm not going to let thoughts of whether or not she is watching stop me. I've come this far and it's completely possible that she is busy with dinner and not paying attention to him at all. I will have time.

It's just a chance I will have to take. I look up at her kitchen, calculating angles. If she glances out of the window, she will only look for him in the tree. She won't think to look down and into the garden of the house behind her. Why would she think to do that? It's where Sam lives. It's no threat to her.

'Hello,' I call one more time, my voice stronger, surer. 'Hello, Riley.'

I am about to call out again when he stops playing the game and looks down at me. 'Oh hey, hello,' he says, and he smiles.

CHAPTER EIGHTEEN
Beverly

Beverly looks out of the kitchen window at Riley who is playing on his iPad. She's glad he doesn't have any homework today. She doesn't want to have to fight to get him to do anything. Using her sleeve, she rubs at her face, removing any remains of her tears as she tries to figure out a way to distract him through the rest of the evening, so that they don't have to have the same conversation again. There are a couple of new movies he wanted to watch and instead of leaving him to it, she will watch with him, she decides. She could make popcorn and snuggle up to him. She glances at her phone lying next to her on the kitchen workbench, willing it to ping with a text from Ethan or for a call to come through. When they were together, he used to call her when he was on his way home from work and they would talk as he made his way through rush-hour traffic. She misses those calls, the idea that at the end of the day there was someone to unwind with, to talk to. But she made the right decision to protect Riley, she knows she did.

I won't work tonight. I'll sit with him and be with him. She glances at the phone again, resentment building inside her. Ethan's punishing her with silence and she's at the point of being glad that she ended the relationship. Who knows what he would have been like a few years into a marriage when life got complicated, because life always got complicated. Her parents were very happy but they had arguments like every other married couple. Her father preferred to take a walk around the block to cool down before he said anything he regretted; Beverly remembers this infuriated her mother who wanted to sort things out right away. She would sit down at the kitchen table with a cup of tea and a crossword puzzle and furiously fill in spaces until her husband returned and they could talk through whatever issue they had. Beverly allows herself a dry laugh as she adds the onions to the pot and stirs them so they brown. She's been like this since she and Ethan broke up. She misses him, she loves him, she resents him, she's angry at him. It's no wonder she's having trouble sleeping. Her emotions are all over the place and the anonymous gifts have only exacerbated things.

Beverly picks some fresh basil from one of the small pots of herbs she is growing on the windowsill and chops it to add it to the sauce. A she does, she sees James doing the same thing for her when she was seventeen, his hands moving rapidly along the chopping board.

'You could have been a chef,' she said to him. It was supposed to be her homework time, but she was mostly scrolling through her phone, looking at Facebook photos. She liked to watch him cook, finding the same peaceful security in watching him work in the kitchen as she had once found in watching her mother.

'You know Georgia is a wonderful cook as well,' he told her. 'Although she doesn't like anything spicy and you know how much I love spicy food.'

Beverly had grabbed a hunk of her long brown hair and inspected it for split ends. 'Yeah, according to you, your girlfriend's wonderful at everything.'

'You should give her a chance, Bev. I like her a lot,' he said, throwing diced capsicum into a wok for the stir-fry he was making them.

Beverly sighed and looked up at the ceiling. 'I find her strange,' she admitted to him.

'What does that mean?' he said.

'I don't know, I just… why do you need to get serious so soon?' *I don't want anyone else here. I don't want you to love anyone else. You're all I've got. Please don't leave me, James. I'm not ready.* All the things she wanted to say were pushed away. Her neediness made her feel stupid and young. She knew she should be happy for her brother but what she mostly was, was jealous. He was all she had left in the world and now he was dividing his time between her and another woman.

James stopped what he was doing and rubbed his head as though she was giving him a headache. 'Listen, Bev, there's something you need to know about Georgia,' he said.

Beverly stood up. She didn't want to talk about her brother's girlfriend, because it felt like they were in some sort of strange competition for James. If she came over to the house, Georgia would drape herself all over James at every opportunity, would pull his attention away from anything to do with Beverly, even if he was trying to help her with her homework. 'Aren't you old enough to figure this out for yourself?' she had said when Beverly asked James to help her come up with ideas for a history project. It was unusual for James to have a girlfriend who didn't at least try to become friendly with Beverly. She didn't like it.

'I don't really want to hear anything else about your beloved Georgia,' she said, snarky and cross with him. 'I'm going round to Sam and Marjorie's place. They said they'll be home in the afternoon with a new puppy and I want to see him.'

'Listen, Bev,' said James, but she had already flounced out of the back door.

*

Beverly shakes her head as she salts the water for the pasta. She hadn't wanted to hear what James was going to tell her, but she probably knew what was coming. She could sense the change in him. He was too protective of the girl. She dismisses the thought and everything that happened after that. She needs to concentrate on Riley now.

Looking out the kitchen window, she sees he's grinning and looking down at something. At least he's happy for the moment. That's all she's ever wanted for him, to just be happy.

CHAPTER NINETEEN

'You're—' he says.

'I am. Hello, Riley.'

'Why are you here in Sam's garden? That's weird. It's a funny place to see you.' He rubs his knee and then sticks his finger in his mouth and paints some spit on the knee.

I take a deep breath, my lie all prepared. 'Well, lucky you, because here I am. I have a new job now.'

'Wow, so quickly. I hurt my knee.' He stretches out his leg so I can see, even though I can't because he's up in the tree and I'm on the ground.

'Sorry,' I say, amazed at how self-centred he is. I need to keep him talking. 'I didn't really like my job at school.'

'Is that 'cause of me and Benji?' He sounds a little sad and I never want him to be sad when he's with me.

'Not at all. I just wanted to do something different. Anyway, I'm Sam's new carer, I'm just here to help him a few days a week until I find something I like better.'

'Oh,' he says, and I see his gaze straying back to the screen. He frowns, unsure about my story but the game quickly draws his attention.

'The thing is,' I say, and he turns to look down at me again, 'I can see you're playing on an iPad and Sam has one that he loves but it's broken, well not broken, but something is wrong with it. He's gone out for a bit and I wanted to fix it for him but I'm struggling with it.'

'Really?' he says. 'Don't you know how to use an iPad?'

'No, I do… I do but sometimes you need a kid to help with these things.'

'That's funny.' He laughs. 'Adults are supposed to be smarter, but they aren't always smarter,' he says. *Such arrogance, such sweet arrogance.* I experience a momentary surge of anger. But then I breathe deeply and let it go. I will have more than enough time to discipline him, to teach him how to be respectful to adults. Obviously Beverly hasn't been doing a very good job. I don't doubt that. She was a child trying to raise a child. A parent should be mature enough to guide their child into the world, not be someone who's still trying to learn how to be in the world themselves. It doesn't matter. I'm here now.

'Yep, you're right about that. Anyway, I was wondering if you would come and take a look at it, since you obviously know everything there is to know about iPads.'

'Okay, just let me tell my mum.' He taps the iPad a few more times and I wait, my impatience growing.

'Oh, I called her and checked with her,' I say quickly. 'She said it's fine as long as you're back in time for dinner.' Another prepared lie. My heart rate increases and I feel a slight flush creeping up my neck. *This has to work. It has to.*

He glances towards the kitchen window as he thinks about this. I look up quickly, relief warm in my blood that she's not looking right at us. She would wonder who he was talking to, but all there is to see in the pane of glass is the framed warm yellow of the kitchen light.

'Okay,' he says and he shoves the iPad in his pants, and almost scampers down the tree, limbs moving over each other rapidly, little pants and grunts accompanying his descent. I want to cheer and clap. I feel like those people who see the finish line of a race and know they are in the lead. I'm almost there. I've almost won.

'You can just climb over here,' I say, keeping my voice deliberately casual.

'I know,' he says, almost rolling his eyes but stopping himself. He doesn't know me well, after all, and I'm pleased to see some manners, not enough but some.

He hands me the iPad and clambers over the fallen tree branch. Then we are both in Sam's garden and he follows me to the house. As we walk, I am holding my breath, expecting that at any moment she will call out and come running. I mentally count the steps to the house, first twenty, then fifteen, then ten, then five, and then I open the back door and we are in the kitchen.

He's only eight so he doesn't say, 'Can you prove you've spoken to my mum?' or 'I've never seen Sam with an iPad,' or 'Sam doesn't have a carer.'

He's only eight so no matter how clever he thinks he is, he's still vulnerable, still powerless against an adult with a plan for him.

When I was about eight, a policeman came to school to give a lecture at our assembly on 'Stranger Danger'.

He told us about all the nefarious ways that bad adults, bad men, will try and entice an innocent boy or girl to come with them. He mentioned candy and puppies and lost cats. He told us about people saying, 'Your mum told me to come and get you.' There was no end to the lies that bad men told to lure young children away to terrible deaths. I bet that policeman never had any idea of what would happen when technology took over the world. He had no idea how easy it would be to find a child or how easily children could be led away. No idea at all.

It's only when I lock the kitchen door behind us that I see a flicker of worry cross Riley's little face. But by then, of course, it's too late.

CHAPTER TWENTY

Beverly

'It's Ethan, leave a message.' Beverly swears under her breath and ends the call. She's not going to leave another message.

It will be time to call Riley in for dinner soon and she wants to be able to tell him she's made a decision. Perhaps she shouldn't worry about it, just give him the Switch and keep him happy, but she knows that if she gives in on something like this, he will read that as weakness. She smiles at this thought. He's only an eight-year-old boy and she's thinking like she's in battle with him. Although sometimes it does feel like she's in a battle of wills with her young son.

She pushes the phone into the pocket of her jeans and walks back over to the stove where the water is boiling for the pasta. As she slides in a handful of spaghetti, she hopes that he will be nice and calm after spending time in his favourite space and perhaps they can have a rational conversation. 'Stop wavering and make a decision,' she tells herself aloud. She would love to be able to tell him that she will get him a Switch for his birthday but it's ridiculously out of her budget. This makes her even angrier with Ethan because it feels like he's showing her up, proving to a child that doesn't even belong to him how much better his life would be if Ethan was still in it.

A streak of anger runs through her, first for the gifts and then for him ignoring her texts and calls. *How dare he?* She looks over at the bottle of wine on the counter, deciding she will have some with dinner, maybe more than a glass, at least enough to relax her so she can stop thinking about Ethan entirely. Her phone pings in her pocket and she feels her heart drop at the conversation she's about to have. She pulls it out and looks at the screen. It's a reminder from the school about the breast cancer fundraiser on tomorrow. The students need to wear something pink and bring a donation. Ethan will be in his car now, on the way home. He's not calling her because he knows it's making things difficult for her.

She picks up a wooden spoon to stir the meat, her heart hammering with fury, making her stir faster than she should, leading to tomato splashes on the stovetop and her pale green shirt. 'Shit,' she mutters and she walks over to the sink to get some paper towel, dampening it and dabbing at the spot on her shirt. She should spray it with stain remover right now. She pulls the shirt up, meaning to toss it in the laundry, but as she does, she looks out of the window and sees that Riley is not up in the tree anymore. She leans forward over the sink and peers into the garden, expecting to see him walking towards the kitchen door, but he's not there. She wouldn't have missed him coming into the house, pretty sure he would have made his presence felt with a slammed door. She goes to the door, opens it and walks out into the garden where the only sound is a lawnmower from a few houses away.

Shivering from the change in temperature, Beverly looks all around the garden and up into the tree again. She steps back and cranes her neck in case he's climbed higher up the branches of the giant old fig tree, even though he's not allowed to. But he's not there and as she moves something crunches underfoot. It's an empty chip packet. She knows he throws down the empty packet to pick up before he comes into the house. He never forgets because he knows that if he does, he won't be allowed to take food up there again. Picking up the packet, she scans the garden again.

The lawnmower stops and there is a moment of silence and, as the wind picks up, something like worry nudges at Beverly.

Walking quickly, she goes back into the house, stopping only to turn off the stovetop so the pasta and sauce don't overcook.

'Riley,' she calls, opening doors as she moves through the house. 'Riley, where are you?'

He's not inside. She opens the front door and looks at the front gate that is closed, the small patch of scraggly grass in the front is empty. 'Riley,' she calls again. She darts out to the street, looks up and down at the parked cars, 'Riley, Riley.' She tries to control the rising panic in her voice but fails. He's here, he has to be here. *Probably in the bathroom.*

She runs back through the house, her heart hammering in her ear, her skin hot in the cool afternoon. She checks her bathroom and his bathroom again. In the back garden she walks around every inch, even though she can see it all, calling him. 'Riley, where are you? Riley, I'm getting worried now, come out please. Riley, Riley, Riley.'

But Riley is gone.

He may have gone next door, but he would never go there without her calling Sam first. She's explained that Sam is an old man and they have to make sure he actually wants a visitor before Riley goes over. She calls Sam anyway, letting the home phone ring for what feels like forever before hanging up and trying his mobile.

'Beverly, love,' Sam answers quickly, 'is everything okay?' She's never called him on his mobile before.

'Oh, Sam, it's… well I can't find Riley, is he over there with you?'

'I'm out, love, been out for a bit. I'm just picking up a few things for dinner at the moment. Should I go home and check? He may have just gone over to play with Scotty. I left him inside, he doesn't like the cold.'

'Oh no… it's fine.' Her voice trails away. She feels ridiculous. How could she have lost her son?

'Scotty will be wanting his dinner soon anyway. I'll go on home and give you a call if he's there. He's just being a bit of a scamp. I remember running away when I was ten… nearly gave my poor mum a heart attack. I packed a suitcase and everything.'

'Oh, thanks, Sam, thanks so much. Ring me if he's there, I'll have my mobile with me.' A small smile creeps across her face. He has probably run away somewhere close, just to scare her. *That's all this is, isn't it? He's just being a bit of a scamp, as Sam said.* But Beverly's smile disappears. Riley has never done anything like this before, and all over a silly device. She is worried again.

Why would he have run away? She doesn't think it's possible that he is even angrier over the game than she realises, but maybe he's even angrier because he thinks it's from Ethan, and now he can't see Ethan anymore. But he was fine when he went outside to climb into his tree. He was happy that she was going to get hold of Ethan and ask about the Switch. *Why would he have left?* Had something, some thought, made him angry again? Did he want to scare her so when he returned, she just gave it to him? *He's not that calculating.* The skin on her arms itches and she scratches. She hopes he's not that calculating. *He's not that calculating, is he?* There are so many things she doesn't know about, so many questions she never got to ask.

If he's taken himself off to the park or to see a friend, he knows that he will get into trouble but perhaps he doesn't care. Flashes of a sixteen-year-old Riley doing a lot of the things she did as a teenager frighten her. *If he's this defiant at eight, what will he be like then?* She can't think about that now. She needs to find him and then he will definitely be sent to his room for a good long think. He can absolutely forget about getting the Switch now.

Before she moves, she closes her eyes and tries to think like an angry eight-year-old boy. *Where might he have gone?* He is friends with Peter, three doors down, and he has been allowed to walk to the park one street away in summer as long as he's with a friend, but he knows that wouldn't be allowed on a school day.

All thoughts of a lovely movie and popcorn night disappear. Beverly runs back inside to grab her jacket before she starts with a visit to the park and then to Peter's house. She thinks about driving to get there quicker but reasons that if she walks or runs, she will see him if he's on the street somewhere.

The last few days, Ethan's gifts, and his subsequent silence, force frustrated tears from her eyes as she leaves the house. She should be living a free and easy life with nothing to do but get herself to work and back. She should have a degree and a nice boyfriend and the ability to go out whenever she wants. Riley has no idea how much she has given up to be his mother, but he's just a little boy. 'Where are you, love?' she mutters, and then she sighs and begins her search.

CHAPTER TWENTY-ONE
Riley

Riley feels weird being in Sam's house without Sam. Scotty is here though and he doesn't seem to mind the woman who says she is Sam's carer. His mum worries about Sam being all alone, so he supposes that having someone to take care of him is a good idea. He likes it when Thea and Amy come to visit their grandfather. He and Thea like to climb the tree together, although she is kind of bossy.

He hunches down and rubs Scotty behind his spiky black ears and the little dog lifts his head in enjoyment.

The woman watches him. Her eyes are green and there is something familiar about her face, but he doesn't know what. Maybe it's because he's seen her at school because she's the lady who has to clean up all the gross stuff like spilled paint and other mess. But it's not just that. He feels like he's seen her somewhere else, not only at school.

She has brown hair and a long fringe, so her eyes are kind of hidden. She is wearing jeans and a red jumper. His mum likes the colour yellow but he likes green. Today his mum is wearing a green shirt but he's still mad at her.

He's going to get into trouble for just leaving the garden but he doesn't care. If she'd let him have the Switch, he could have beaten like a hundred levels by now. Well, maybe not a hundred, but he could definitely have beaten some. He's trying to not get angry about the Switch again, but every time he thinks about it his ears feel hot and he wants to shout at someone. Ethan would have been a good dad for him and he, for sure, would have bought him lots more good presents. He sighs and looks up at the woman. There are too many things to think about and he doesn't want to think about any of them. The woman is just watching him, her green eyes wide in her face.

He doesn't know why she's locked the kitchen door. Or why she has such a strange smile on her face. Maybe he really should have talked to his mum, but it's too late now and he doesn't know why that makes him feel a little strange, like he felt when he was going to the doctor for a sore throat and he thought that he was going to get an injection. He still remembers his vaccinations from when he was five and they hurt. Nothing in Sam's house can hurt him so he doesn't know why he has the weird butterfly feeling in his stomach. There's nothing to worry about here.

CHAPTER TWENTY-TWO

'So, where's the iPad?' he asks, uncertainty in his voice. He's wondering if he's made a mistake. He has no idea who I am, beyond that I arrived with a mop and bucket when there was spilled paint in his classroom and that I waved to him crossing the playground. I haven't even offered him my name. He and his little friend didn't ask for it either when they helped me clean up the paint. No one asks the cleaner their name. No one looks at the person who has to deal with all the things they would rather not deal with.

I am studying his face, wishing I could get closer and touch him. His hair is cut short so I can see that there is a slight shadow just near his left eye. It's a strawberry birthmark. They fade as you get older and on him it's so small you can barely see it. Mine was bigger when I was a child, but it's faded now as well. Genetics is a funny thing. It's amazing what gets inherited.

When I first saw his picture on Facebook, I felt the shock of absolute recognition, but I wasn't certain, not completely certain. Until I enlarged the picture and saw the mark, the little mark that makes him the baby I held and wanted to hold forever. He was so light but so solid at the same time. Completely in the world and yet not strong enough to hold up his head. Babies are so vulnerable. I know that I vowed to protect him when he was in my arms, to always love and protect him, and I would have if not for her. *Lying, stealing bitch.* But there is no time for those kinds of thoughts now. I need to get him out of the kitchen and into the basement.

'It's just down here,' I say, walking in front of him so that he feels less threatened. 'Follow me.' I keep my tone light and my movements casual. Once he's in the basement it will be easy to deal with him and then I can explain without him leaving. I can explain again and again until he understands and then I can take the necessary steps to make sure he comes home with me. Not just home with me, but home to my parents as well, to his grandparents.

He will be happy to have grandparents. I know that he doesn't think he has any now. Beverly's parents died in a car crash. I heard that story often enough, nodded my head in seeming sympathy even though I was secretly thinking that it must be nice to have your parents simply disappear from your life for good, leaving you all their money and a house.

But after he arrived, I knew that grandparents were an important thing for a child, another generation to help nurture and love them. It will be a wonderful discovery for him. For them too. There is a sharp stab in my heart as I think of my parents and I feel like there is something I should remember, something to do with them. I rub my forehead, rubbing away any negative thoughts. I am within reach of my goal now. I don't need to ruin everything with negative thinking.

Whatever happened between us is in the past, and my parents will be happy to see me now. I know they will. All through our childhood, my sister and I understood that my parents didn't want children but one night, when we were sixteen and fifteen, my father had too much to drink and instead of it making him vicious and angry as it usually did, it made him maudlin. He had spent the day drinking in a pub to celebrate his friend's son leaving for Iraq after joining the army. My father couldn't stop talking about how nice the young man was, how proud his dad was of him and how everyone in the pub had looked at both the father and the son with so much respect.

'Bart has every right to be proud of that boy, I'm telling you,' he told us all over dinner as he consumed his tenth or eleventh beer. 'He's a good boy and he's off to do an important job.'

My mother was sipping her wine slowly, her lips thin with disapproval at his inebriated conversation, but at this she nodded. 'Well, of course it's all worth it if you have a son, isn't it? I mean it all would have been different if we'd had the chance to raise a boy. He would have been a fine young man. Girls can be so...' and here she studied my sister and me, 'bitchy,' she finished and took a huge gulp of her wine. She smiled, the hurtful words making her happy.

'Too right,' my father said, sniggering. Neither my sister nor I had the guts to point out that she was the bitch.

Her comment about raising a boy shocked me. I always imagined that children in general were not to her taste. It was disconcerting to learn that it wasn't children so much as the gender of those children that upset my parents. My sister smirked because by then she had developed the gift of disdain when it came to my parents. 'Bitter, twisted old drunks,' is how she referred to them if we ever had a civil conversation. But I was still hoping for some connection and I looked down at my roast chicken, knowing that I wouldn't be able to swallow another bite. It wasn't that they hadn't wanted children at all. It was that they had wanted a son. It didn't matter how perfect, how amazing, my sister and I tried to be – we would never be good enough. There was, I have to admit, some comfort in the idea that my beautiful, clever sister would always let them down because she wasn't a boy. Some comfort but not enough.

I should never see my parents again. I should understand that they never loved me and that nothing I can do will make them love me. But the logic of this does not transcend my damaged heart. I want to turn up on their doorstep with the longed-for son. I want to call them right now to tell them the news, but I know

I have to wait until everything is in place. I want to be the one to bring them the thing they actually wanted. Nothing my sister ever achieves or achieved could top that. As I think about calling them, I mentally recite my old home phone number in my head and something niggles at me again but I dismiss it. Eight years ago, I planned to return home, triumphant with a beautiful son. That was the plan and it's still the plan now. Beverly thinks she's won but she hasn't. She merely interrupted the plan, sending it slightly off course. It's back on track now.

I walk towards the back of the basement, as though looking for the iPad, and he follows me, Scotty at his heels.

'It's over here somewhere,' I say, my heart thrumming with excitement. 'It's over here,' I repeat and he and Scotty follow me all the way to the back wall where there is an old timber desk piled with stuff. Sam is a big collector of books and the basement is lined with shelves stacked high with them, all growing slightly mouldy because it's damp down here. There are lots of books on the desk as well as brown folders with labels like: *House Insurance* and *Car Insurance* and *Bank Account Details*. Sam's whole life is on display down here. I looked through the bank account details and he has a reasonable sum of money. I'm not going to steal anything from him because I'm not that kind of person, but I have copied down the details just in case I need them. I will look at it as a gift from him for helping take care of Scotty sometimes. He's old and has no need for so much money and Liza doesn't need the money either.

I stand with my hands on my hips, looking at the desk, shaking my head with dramatic frustration. It looks like the iPad could be here under all this stuff. It really looks like it could.

'I need to clean this up,' I mutter. 'Sam told me he put it on the desk but who can see anything in this mess?'

'Yeah, you're right,' Riley laughs. And then he steps forward, right next to me, so close I can feel the heat coming from his body and smell the soap he must use to wash his hands. It takes everything I have inside me to prevent my hands from moving towards him, but I know I need to wait. He starts pushing books aside and I thrill with joy. *I've got him.*

CHAPTER TWENTY-THREE

Beverly

'I'm sorry, he's not here,' says Peter's mother, Lindy. 'You'd tell Beverly if you'd seen Riley, wouldn't you, love?' she says to her son who is standing next to his mother, a half-chewed apple in his hand.

'Uh-huh,' says Peter and he takes another bite of his apple. Lindy rubs his head affectionately and Beverly can actually see her thanking God that she is not the mother running around the neighbourhood looking for her lost son. But of course she wouldn't be *that* mother. Lindy's blonde hair is in a neat, low ponytail and she is wearing a flowered apron over her black jeans and white collared shirt to make dinner. Beverly knows an apron is sensible, and she has one, but she feels ridiculous putting it on, as though she's an old woman. From inside Lindy's house the smell of something rich and meaty cooking is obvious, and Beverly experiences a momentary pang of jealousy at Lindy's neat life and her sweet child standing next to her. She has run all the way from her house and she knows her hair is a curly mess and her cheeks are bright red from the cold and the worry that is flowing through her veins like blood.

'Perhaps he's just gone for a little walk,' Lindy says helpfully and she puts an arm around Peter's shoulders, pulls him a little closer to her. 'Do you want us to come and help you look? Peter's a really fast runner.' She starts to turn around as if to get her coat but Beverly doesn't want her helping. Embarrassment makes her refuse. *What kind of a mother loses her child?*

'Um, no… no, I'm sure I'll find him soon. He's a bit cross with me over, you know gaming and things. He's probably already at home and wondering where his dinner is.' She smiles and Lindy tries for a smile but she can see the concern on the woman's face.

'Well, let us know if you want some help,' she says. 'And do let me know when you've found him.'

Beverly nods and makes her way out into the street again. She has already checked the park and he's not there. She has no idea where else he could be.

The sun is beginning to set and it will be dark soon, the wind is chilly but she's sweating in her jacket, hot from running and panic. This is not like him. He's never done something like this before and as she walks, peering into gardens, and at windows where lights are turning on, beaming yellow in the afternoon gloom, she knows that all her worries about him have been leading to something like this happening. *Where are you, my little boy?* Places he could be fly rapidly through her head, each one quickly dismissed for one reason or another. Benji is his best friend but it's a long walk to his house. The shopping centre is one of his favourite places because of the arcade but that's closed now. The skatepark would still be filled with kids, even on a winter afternoon, but his skateboard is still by the front door. He's only wearing shorts and a jumper and it's getting too cold to be outside dressed like that. An involuntary shiver ripples through Beverly as she thinks of him in the chilly air.

Her mind strays back to her brother James, as it always does when she has no idea which way to turn. If he were here right now, he would know where to look and what to do. He always seemed to know how to handle a situation, whereas even now, as a mother with a child, she still feels like she's floundering. After their parents died, she knows she made his life difficult. She was in trouble at school all the time and, more than once, she'd had to call him in the middle of the night to pick her up from a party that even she, despite how drunk she was, could see was out of control. James always came. He would take her home and put her to bed, leaving water and Panadol next to her for when she woke up, dry-mouthed with a thumping head. In the morning he would lecture her about the dangers of binge drinking and going to parties with young men she didn't really know. Even as she rolled her eyes, she hoped he knew she was grateful. It felt like there was still a parent in the house. Her aching loneliness for her mother often kept her awake all night, wishing that things were different, praying that they could be, as if wishes and prayers could bring her mother back, her gold-brown hair loosely tied back and her body swaying in the kitchen as she hummed a tune while cooking. 'How's tricks?' she would ask Beverly every afternoon when she picked her up from school, and it never failed to make Beverly smile, even on the bad days. James tried to fill the void. He took an interest in her studying and would listen to long rambling stories about her school friends, even though she knows he must have been bored rigid. He was working all day and keeping up with the shopping and the cooking and the cleaning, and while she tried to help a little, she knows she was selfish as she dealt with her grief and her anger at the unfairness of it all. James was patient and kind and held her while she cried when it was all too much.

That's what made his relationship with Georgia seem strange to her. The honeymoon period of their relationship was over quickly and his face stopped lighting up when he talked about her. Georgia became demanding, sometimes irrational. She wanted to move into the house, to get married and start a family. James never told Beverly any of this, but she became adept at listening to them argue in the living room when she was supposed to be in her room doing homework or scrolling through her phone.

*

'If you loved me enough,' Georgia had told James one night, 'you would have proposed already. I want my parents to see me married and they're getting old.'

James had thought Georgia was beautiful, with wide green eyes and long brown hair, but Beverly saw something else when she looked at her, something under the surface, something simmering, something calculating.

Beverly was listening into their conversations because she had become convinced that if they did get married, Georgia would make sure that she got pushed out of the house. She didn't understand the relationship because they were so different. James was laid-back and got along with everyone but every time she came over, Georgia always had a new story about someone who had upset her by saying or doing the wrong thing. She got into arguments with shop assistants and co-workers all the time. James liked nothing more than a movie night on the sofa, but Georgia wanted to go out all the time and eat in expensive restaurants. James wasn't ready for marriage and Georgia was obsessed with it.

'I do love you, George, I promise. I just want to give Bev a bit more time,' she heard James say to her that night.

'She's had all the time she needs. She's nearly finished school. Perhaps it's time she found a place of her own. Your parents left her some money – she could use it for rent.'

Beverly had been standing outside the living room, concealed by a wall, feeling sneaky. She hadn't stayed to listen to anything else. Instead, she had stomped off to her room so they could be sure she'd heard them, as hot tears fell. She wasn't going to let Georgia push her out of her own house and she didn't think James would allow it to happen either, but she had moments of being unsure about that. She was hard work, she knew she was, and sometimes she saw her brother looking at her and she wondered if he was thinking how much easier his life would be if he didn't have an emotional, grief-stricken teenager hanging around. He was still dealing with his own grief. She resented the fact that he had someone he loved and she kept looking for something like that with the boys she slept with, hoping to make some kind of connection with one of them. She rarely used protection and now she knows that at some point she thought, *Well, so what if I get pregnant? I'll always have someone who loves me then.*

She disliked Georgia more with each passing day.

James's previous girlfriends had always made an effort with her, asking her about school or her own friends, but Georgia looked at her like she was in the way.

'You don't go out much,' she would say, smiling. 'Don't you have any friends?' Beverly gritted her teeth and hated the woman who, at thirty-two, was five years older than James.

'Shouldn't you be dating someone your own age?' Beverly once threw back at her.

'Temper, temper,' Georgia had laughed.

The longer James and Georgia were together, the more unhappy he looked but he never wanted to admit that he was unhappy. Beverly pushed him, criticising Georgia and telling him he could do better:

'I never thought you'd land up with a woman who hates country music.' … 'How come she never helps you clean up after you've cooked dinner – just sits there and watches you?' … 'She really seems to hate me. It feels like she doesn't want you to pay attention to anyone but her.' … 'That girl at the coffee shop we go to asked about you today – she's got a real crush on you and she's just gorgeous.'

Driving a wedge between them became something Beverly focused on. It stopped her thinking about her own pain and sadness. She regrets that behaviour now, is horrified at how selfish she was. But no matter what she said James never wanted to listen to her. Georgia drove him crazy, but he was completely in love with her. He had so many excuses for her:

'She's had a difficult life.' … 'Her parents were abusive.' … 'She has no one to turn to but me.' … 'She was hit a lot.' … 'She hasn't learned to let herself be loved.' … 'All she wants is a family and security.'

'If her parents were so terrible, why does she want them to see her get married?' Beverly had asked him one evening.

'How do you know she said that?' James replied, his eyes narrowing with suspicion.

Beverly shrugged her shoulders, not caring that she had outed herself as spying.

'Oh, Bev,' he sighed. 'It's complicated. She wants them to be proud of her, I guess, to see that she's done something good with her life. She wanted to go to university but her grades in the last year of school weren't good enough and her parents kicked her out as soon as she was old enough, and all the dreams she had for herself have kind of…' He waved his hands in the air.

'You get that you can't make up for her shitty parents by marrying her, right?' Beverly told him.

'I do,' he said, 'but, Bev… the thing is… the thing is…' He stopped speaking.

They were sitting on the sofa together, eating their Indian takeaway off plates they held while watching a movie. Beverly waited, taking another mouthful of her creamy korma and then sipping some of her Coke before she realised that he hadn't finished his sentence.

'The thing is what?' she asked, turning to look at him.

He put his plate down on the coffee table and wiped his mouth before taking a long drink of his beer. 'Georgia's pregnant.'

Beverly put her plate down on the table as well, her appetite instantly gone, the korma turning sludgy in her mouth. 'Pregnant?' she said, refusing to believe the word, refusing to confront everything that word meant for her and her life. The way he said it, the finality in his voice, let her know that a decision had already been made. Beverly looked around the living room at the cream-coloured walls adorned with photographs and two of her mother's inexpert landscapes. The room suddenly felt small and she knew it was because soon the house would not be big enough for her to go on living there.

'Yes,' he nodded – she noticed his hair was too long again and his eyes were a little bloodshot, 'pregnant.'

And, just like her world had shifted on the day she learned her parents were dead, Beverly had felt her world shift again.

Beverly pushes her hair behind her ears, hating the way the wind keeps blowing it into her face, and she lets go of any thoughts of James. She's alone now, she has been for a long time, and she needs to find her son.

She makes her way back home. Riley is nowhere but she walks through the house again, looking everywhere, even in the large cupboard in her bedroom because when he was little, he used to hide in there.

She hurries back to the kitchen, holding an image of him sitting at the table and hoping that he will grin and say, 'I'm starving, what's for dinner?' But the kitchen is empty, the house is empty and the garden, shrouded in darkness, reveals nothing in the beam of a torch she takes to march around the edges.

Riley is simply gone.

CHAPTER TWENTY-FOUR

While he's busy sifting through the detritus on the desk, I say, 'Oh, I forgot,' and I dart back up the stairs and lock the basement door. I don't explain what I forgot but I move quickly enough so he doesn't have time to process what's happening. The lock makes a heavy, satisfying click and I push the key deep into the pocket of my jeans. As I come down the stairs, slowly so I can enjoy his realisation, he backs away from me, his eyes scanning the room for an escape. Because now he knows. There is a small lurch of sympathy for him inside me because on his face I read fear, confusion and disbelief all at once.

'Look,' I say, because I can see his body tensing, his eyes shining with the beginning of tears, 'you don't need to be afraid of me.' I move slowly towards him, even as he moves along the wall, his back sliding on the timber panelling.

'Stop moving,' I command, and he does.

'I want to go home,' he says, scowling. He crosses his arms, protecting himself, still hoping that his demands will be met. 'There's no iPad here, you're a liar.' His voice rises just a little and I can see that this is probably how he deals with situations when he's angry. He shouts. He hasn't yelled at me but he's working his way up to it, testing the waters to see how I'll react. I was never allowed to shout. Shouting earned a smack, hard and so fast it took your breath away. Something else I'm going to have to teach him.

'I want to go home. My mum is probably calling me.' He bites down on his lip, moderating his voice, and I can see that he's being cautious. He's not sure how to deal with me, but he doesn't have to worry about that because I know exactly how to deal with him.

Scotty is next to him and he bends down and picks up the little dog, holding him like a comfort toy. Scotty licks his nose, delighted to be cuddled. 'You're a liar,' he says again and he looks at the stairs. I have taken a few steps away from the staircase and I can see the wheels of his mind churning, planning. He can't do anything. The key is in my pocket, the lock solid and strong. Whoever built the house may have meant this basement to be a room to rent out or a place where things could be safely stored. Sam left the door unlocked, probably has left the door unlocked for years, but helpful Liza had labelled the key for him.

Another stab of sympathy for the boy makes me cough. He has no idea who he's dealing with or that what he's planning is transparently obvious on his face. He takes a small step forward towards the stairs and I stifle a laugh. He's being silly but I don't want to tell him that. He won't believe me unless I show him and I will show him.

He puts the dog down and starts to move towards the basement stairs, his eyes on me as if daring me to try and stop him.

I hold up my hands. 'Now listen, Riley. I'm not going to hurt you…'

He rushes forward, but I'm quicker and I'm instantly in front of the stairs. He charges into my body with all his strength. 'Oof,' I say as he makes contact and I stagger backwards a step or two. He pushes past me, panting, and runs up the stairs but I regain my balance and I race after him, grabbing him by his jumper from behind and pulling him, making him trip down the steps with a couple of thumps.

'Ow,' he shouts, 'let go, let go, let go of me. Help, help.' He kicks his legs and tries to grab my hands to pull them off him but I'm stronger than he is. I drag him back further and then I put my arms around him and lift. He's heavy and tough to handle his feet kicking and his whole body wriggling. I push my hand across his mouth, cupping it a little to stop him from biting me like he's trying to do. I struggle over to the sofa with him and then I dump him onto the cushions, pushing him down and grabbing the knife I have hidden behind one of the brown throw pillows. It's a large kitchen knife with a worn wooden handle but the blade is still sharp with the promise of what it can do. Sam uses it to slice easily through chunks of chicken before he cooks them up for Scotty to have as a treat.

I hold the knife right next to Riley's face, and all movement ceases. His eyes widen, his mouth opens in shock and fear makes him tremble. He backs away, further into the sofa, trying to disappear into the pillows.

'Now listen,' I say, panting slightly. 'I don't want to hurt you. I just want to talk to you. I need to explain things about your mum and dad. All I want you to do is listen to me, but if you don't or if you won't, I will hurt you. Do you understand?'

The light is on in the basement as it always is, because very little light comes in from the long narrow window at the top of one wall, and I move the knife back and forth, enjoying the way the yellow beam glints off the steel blade.

Horror is etched across his face and I feel bad, well not bad really, more irritated. I need him to stop fighting me so I can talk to him. I need time to explain it all and then the knife and my threats will no longer be necessary. I hope.

I grab the zip ties I have shoved in my pocket and show them to him. They are made of thin black plastic and don't look strong enough to hold his hands together, but I know they work.

'If you move, I'll tie you up and it won't feel nice, okay? And if you move, I'll have to hurt you with this,' I say, holding the knife just above his head. 'I don't want to hurt you, Riley, so you need to promise me that you won't try to run away again. The basement door is locked and I will catch you. I know you understand that.

I will catch you.' I try to moderate my tone. I don't want him to hate me, just to behave. A moment when my mother used her hairbrush to hit me across the face comes to me: 'All I want is for you to behave. Why is that so hard for you?' she had screamed. I never thought I would understand my mother, but I am starting to. She had her reasons for what she did. Children who are undisciplined are difficult for everyone. I will not have a difficult child.

'Okay,' he says and a tear makes its way down his cheek. Scotty jumps up onto the sofa and crawls onto his lap, the tiny dog sensing that he needs him.

'Oh, Riley, don't cry,' I say, my heart melting a little at his distress, 'it's going to be fine. I'm just here to tell you the truth about everything.'

I sit down on the sofa, one seat cushion away from him. I rest my hands in my lap, clutching the knife tightly. I watch him closely as I rehearse what I'm going to say to him for the thousandth time. I want the moment to be perfect, for it to be exactly how I have seen it in my head. I don't know if I will hurt him and that worries me. I might. I might and that worries me quite a lot. I can picture the knife slicing his cheek, the blood that would appear. I can see my hands around his thin neck as I watch his eyes bulge. I shake the thoughts away. *I'm not going to hurt him. I am not my parents.*

When I was growing up, I understood that I was hurt by my parents because I was bad, because I was a constant disappointment. I believed they loved my sister better and even though she was hurt by them as well, I thought that she knew they loved her over me. Years later, when my sister came back into my life, we had moments where we would speak openly with each other and from what she told me, I understood that she didn't believe my parents loved or respected her at all. History is very much all about perspective. Once I left home and went out into the world and met more people, I understood that my parents were the problem and not me. I'm a nice person, and after I left home, my face and body changed and when I looked in the mirror, I no longer saw an ungainly, ugly girl but rather a pretty woman with big green eyes. There have been a lot of men in my life, but even the men I loved never loved me enough to make up for what's missing in my heart, for the gaping hole caused by a mother and a father incapable of love. I had hoped to find a husband to love me one day; I hoped, but I failed at that.

I feel like I have tried to be a better person than my parents thought I was, than what they raised me to be. But it's possible that the damage they did, the damage that I haven't been able to shake off, means that I could hurt him, I could hurt this little boy. *My little boy.* I could hurt him because I have hurt others. It was never my fault, because how can I be blamed for something that was beaten into me? But still, I don't think I want to hurt him. Discipline him, yes, hurt him, no. Perhaps that was all my parents wanted as well but it always felt more like they enjoyed causing us pain. They won't be like that as grandparents, I'm sure.

He is watching me, his hands stroking Scotty compulsively, slowly.

'What… what are you going to tell me the truth about?' he asks, eyeing the knife. His voice is high with distress, the words ending in held-back tears.

'Your mum,' I say simply.

'What about my mum?' he asks and he cannot help showing some curiosity. He rubs one eye and sniffs. Now is not the time for him to cry, not when he's interested in what I have to say. I smile because this is going exactly the way I wanted it to go.

'She's been keeping a secret from you,' I say, a spark of joy flaring inside me. I can't wait for the big reveal. I know he's going to be so happy to have the truth, to know who I am and what I am to him.

'My mum doesn't keep secrets,' he scoffs and I sense his waning interest as though I have said something ridiculous.

'This is such a big secret, such an enormous secret, that she had to keep it.' I say it as though I am telling him an exciting story. I run my finger up and down the blade of the knife, nicking my skin a little. 'Ouch,' I say, sucking the tiny drop of blood that had appeared. His eyes widen.

He doesn't ask what the secret is, instead looking down at the dog as he rubs behind his ears.

I want him to ask, I need him to ask. I have rehearsed this moment, seen how it would go. I need him to ask so that when I reveal the truth, he will direct his anger towards her, will never want to see her again and then I will be there to comfort, to love, to mother him.

'My mum doesn't keep secrets,' he whispers, repeating the words more to himself than to me.

'Oh, but she does, Riley, and the biggest secret she's been keeping, the most terrible one, is that…' I pause for effect. My mother used to tell me that I was overly dramatic, an insult that barely had the power to hurt after everything else. In the silence he looks up at me and I can see him gritting his teeth to prevent himself from asking. I decide to tell him anyway. He needs to know.

'The secret is that she is not actually your mum at all.'

CHAPTER TWENTY-FIVE

Beverly

Beverly calls the police, her hands shaking so much that she hits the wrong digits twice. 'My son is missing,' she says when a woman answers the phone. The word 'missing' steals her breath. Because she can feel that this is not just a cross little boy who has run away, although she doesn't know why she is so certain of this. *Would Ethan steal her son away?* The idea is ludicrous. But now she can feel that this is the beginning of something bigger than she can deal with, but also that everything she has been hiding, all the secrets she has been keeping, are about to come to light. How will she explain it all? Police ask questions. There will be so many questions. The fear of slipping up, of letting out a tiny bit of truth that leads to a cracking open of her whole lie, is always with her.

While she waits for the police, she hunts out Riley's birth certificate because they will want to see that. The authorities always do.

The night he was born it was cold and dark by 5 p.m. A birth at home was the plan but no one had expected so much blood or the level of pain. When it was over, Beverly had held him in her arms and felt the wonderment of a new soul in the world. 'Hello, you,' she had whispered to him. 'Hello.' He had stretched out a little hand and she had touched her finger to it, been surprised by how tightly he gripped her finger. His grey eyes, that would soon turn green, blinked as he focused on her face, their gazes meeting for a moment, and she felt a rush, a pull, a yank of love inside her.

He was so present, so here in the world when only a moment before he hadn't been. All the worry she had been feeling over his arrival disappeared. She didn't know it was possible to fall instantly and completely in love, but she had.

She places the birth certificate on the coffee table. And she begins a list of places he might be, people the police should speak to, doors she thinks they should knock on even though she has already done all this. She's called Sam, visited Peter, looked in the park. *Where else could he be?* She writes down ideas she has discarded, just in case.

The list is short and doesn't take her long, and then she has to sit on her hands to fight the urge to leave the house and run around the neighbourhood again. She mentally rehearses answers to the questions she might be asked. She remembers a night when he was five and his temperature shot up suddenly, his ear turning red as he clutched it. 'It hurts, Mum, it hurts.' She had given him Panadol and held him on her lap but after half an hour, his temperature still hadn't gone down. Panic had gripped her as she ran him out to the car and drove to the nearest hospital emergency room. 'It'll be okay, it'll be okay,' she repeated the whole way as Riley's face flushed and his eyes glazed over.

At the hospital she had been rushed through and then had wanted to scream with frustration when the doctor on duty began questioning her. 'And did you have any problems with his birth?' the young woman had asked as she filled in a form.

'What? No, why does that matter? It's an ear infection,' Beverly said.

'Sorry, they're just standard questions.'

Standard questions that other mothers never had to think about haunted Beverly.

'How long was your labour? Does he look like his dad? Who's your obstetrician? Did you breastfeed? Why not?' Questions mothers asked each other in casual conversation made Beverly seem distant and cold when she stumbled over answers or didn't reply.

Now, hours or only minutes pass and then the doorbell rings. Her heart hammers in her chest, her mouth is dry. She has no idea what's going to happen next. 'Please come home, Riley,' she whispers as she stands up and walks to her front door.

CHAPTER TWENTY-SIX

Riley stares at me, every inch of him a study in scepticism. His arms are crossed, his feet twisted together, his eyes narrowed and a scowl on his face. I assumed he would just believe me. I don't have much experience with eight-year-old boys. I should have eight years of experience. I remember holding him when he was a baby, the lovely biscuit smell of him, the way he settled when he was crying and I picked him up. I was born to be a mother. That chance should not have been taken from me, but today I take it back.

'That's just rubbish,' he says.

'Not rubbish, Riley, it's the truth. She's not your mum at all; in fact, she stole you from your real mum…' I hesitate, 'me,' I say quietly, and then louder, with more certainty, 'me.' A series of images that I have held on to in the last year come to me. I have nurtured them, filled out the details, run them through my mind on repeat. An image of me walking into school with him holding my hand, 'Your son looks exactly like you,' a woman with blonde hair says and Riley smiles as I smile, our gazes meet, and we laugh in the sunshine. An image of me opening the door to a visiting friend, an apron around my waist. 'Your mum is the best,' says the little boy as I give Riley and his friend a home-made cupcake. And the best image, the one where I turn up on my parents' doorstep and ring the bell. I can see my mother opening the door, her face settled into lines and wrinkles, her lips still thin and her grey hair cut in a short bob. 'What are you doing here?' she will ask, her voice dry of love or concern. 'I'm here to show you something,' I reply and then Riley steps out from behind me.

'This is Riley, my son, your grandson,' I say and she looks down at him, tears fill her pale green eyes and spill over.

'Douglas, Douglas, come and see, come and see,' she will call to my father who will appear with his paunch only slightly straining against his belt, his grey beard neat and tidy.

'Our grandson,' my mother says, as Riley gives them a cheeky smile.

And then we are both hugged and ushered inside their home where we all live together happily. I have trouble making the last image work sometimes, something keeps getting in the way, but I'm sure it's only because I haven't seen my parents properly for a long time. Perhaps they look different now and that's why the image gives me trouble. But in each of the images, one thing remains the same: Riley. His green eyes, lighter than mine but still green, and his cheeky smile, and his absolute love and adoration of me. Except, right now, he is not behaving the way he should. I've revealed something wonderful and he's still looking at me as though he's not happy. He should be overjoyed. *Why isn't he overjoyed?*

He laughs and then shakes his head. 'I think you're mad,' he says quietly. 'And you're bad because it's bad to tell a lie. You lied about Sam having an iPad so you must be lying about this as well.'

He rubs at the side of his eye and I lean forward to touch his face so I can feel the small birthmark, the same way I sometimes touch mine, just to know it's there. He rears back, pushing himself further away from me. I need to take this slowly but irritation is flaring inside me. I've told him the truth and he's a child and children should believe everything their parents say.

'Your birthday is in August,' I say. I'm going to tell him everything I know about him.

'My whole class knows that,' he sneers. 'Actually my whole school does because every morning at assembly they make birthday announcements.' He folds his arms, proud of having caught me out.

I put the knife down on the sofa next to me so that he doesn't have to be scared. Children should not fear their parents, but they should respect them. I'm his mother and he should believe what I say because of that, but I can see he will be more difficult to convince than I thought. Before I launch into the truth there is the sound of the front door opening upstairs. Footsteps above tell me Sam's home.

'Hello, Scotty, where are you, boy, come on,' he calls. He is unused to Scotty not greeting him immediately. The little dog stands up on the sofa, his triangular ears moving back and forth and then he jumps off and scampers up the basement stairs to Sam, giving a little bark at the locked door.

'Just—' I start to say but there's no way Riley's listening to me.

'Help,' he shouts, standing up. 'Help, Sam, help, it's Riley.' He scrambles over the back of the sofa and runs up the basement stairs.

Scotty starts barking, a mad continuous bark, and Sam yells, 'What? Who said that? Riley? Riley, where are you? Scotty, Scotty, what's going on?'

'I'm here, Sam, in the basement, help.' He takes the stairs two at a time but I follow him up, quicker than I knew I could. I grab the back of his shirt, just as the door handle to the basement begins to turn. Scotty barks and barks and Sam starts pulling the door as he twists the handle.

'Scotty, Riley, are you two locked in? Are you locked in? What's going on?' calls Sam through the door.

I drag Riley back down the stairs again, his feet flailing so he doesn't trip, and I shove him on the sofa. The alarm of being caught, of being found out before I have managed to convince him, forces my heart to pound in my chest, anxiety heating my blood. This is not what was supposed to happen. I pull my arm back to deliver him a mighty slap but restrain myself. I clench my fist instead and wave it in front of his face so he knows what I can do, what I'm willing to do. 'I wish you hadn't done that,' I spit. 'Now stay there or I will hurt you.'

He stares at me, absolute shock on his face as tears trace their way down his cheeks as he cowers in a corner of the sofa. Beverly probably never hits him. I have always believed that I would never hit my child but I can see that my parents may have been right about some things. Children need to listen to their parents. A disciplined child is a happy child and I will not have my child acting out.

I pick up the mallet that I have taken from Sam's shed. It will be a shame if he doesn't survive being hit on the head. I didn't want to have to do this, but I knew it was a possibility that Sam would find me here at some point. The mallet was at the back of his shed, lying on a wooden bench. I took it because it always helps to have a plan B. Plan A was that Sam wouldn't find out I was here until I had spirited my son away. Plan B is what I have to do if he does.

He is still turning the handle and pulling at the locked door shouting, 'Riley, Riley.' He's only a moment away from calling Beverly or the emergency services. I can feel it. Scotty's barking is driving me mad. 'Shut up, Scotty,' I shout as I sprint up the stairs and open the door. Scotty dashes out, running circles around Sam.

He steps back, his mouth open, his face pale with shock, 'What—' he begins and I step forward and swing the mallet before he has time to process what's happening. He drops to the floor and lies still. Scotty is barking at me, his body bouncing with indignation, teeth bared.

'Shh, Scotty,' I try, moderating my tone. The poor little dog doesn't like being yelled at but he needs to be quiet. 'Stop,' I say forcefully but he keeps going, the sound ricocheting in my head. He won't stop. I lift my hand to swing the mallet again but Riley shouts from the bottom of the stairs.

'No… no… please, Scotty, come here, boy, come here, Scotty!'

The dog dashes past me and down the stairs, leaping into Riley's waiting arms.

'Shh, boy, shh, it's okay,' he whispers to the dog.

His tear-stained face is more irritating than heartbreaking. I admit that I thought I would feel a rush of love when I was finally near him, the same way I did when he was a baby, but I haven't seen him for such a long time. I hope that something deep and primal kicks in because you need to be able to love a child to be a mother, although I suppose my mother didn't really love me. Perhaps she will love Riley more.

'See that you keep him quiet,' I say, making sure the menace in my voice conveys my message.

I look down at Sam. There is a slight trickle of blood coming from a small cut on his forehead but what's more worrying is the skin on the side of his face that is blackening and puffing up. I should not have hit him that hard and I squeeze my eyes shut and wish I could take that action back. I'm not actually here to hurt anyone – well, one person, but she deserves it. She'll understand why I'm doing it. I'm trying to reunite a family and I'm trying to give my parents a gift. I'm trying to have just one moment in the sun as the favourite child, and now it's all getting difficult and complicated because he wouldn't just let me explain. Because he wouldn't believe me.

Riley backs away from the stairs and sits down on the sofa with the dog in his arms. He leans forward and whispers into his black silky ear, but I don't worry about that. I lean down and grab Sam under his shoulders and I drag him down the steps into the basement. He is heavier than I thought he would be and the effort of trying to keep him from bumping too hard on the stairs is making me sweat and pant, but finally he is in the basement lying on the floor.

I sit on the bottom step with my head in my hands looking at the old man.

'You killed him,' says Riley, his voice thick with despair, and I look at him and see that he's crying again. I don't think I cried this much as a child.

I lean down and check Sam's pulse which is weak but still there. 'I didn't. He's still alive.' I stand up. I need to think this through without any distractions. I'm not sure what I'm going to do now. I thought I would explain the whole thing to Riley and he would be grateful to come away with me. I probably didn't think it through enough. My mother is right, I make stupid, impulsive decisions, I leap before I look and I never consider all the angles. I feel like crying myself, but there's no way I'm doing that in front of a child. I need some space, some time away from this mess so I can think clearly.

'I'm going to leave for a bit,' I tell him. 'There's a bathroom behind you if you need it.'

'I know,' he sneers, his tears disappearing. 'Sam and Scotty are my friends.' He puts the dog down and stares at me defiantly, his hands clenched into fists. I want to laugh at him. I can see myself as a child standing up to the schoolyard bully. I got into fights a lot as a girl, far too much. I would come home with a black eye from school when I was ten and eleven and receive a beating from my father. 'What. Kind. Of. A. Girl. Gets. Into. Fights,' he would say as his hand holding the belt swung back and forth, his breath heavy with the effort of making sure the leather came down hard enough on my skin to leave red welts even through my clothes.

'You're a terrible disappointment,' my mother would say after my father was done and I was collapsed on the floor of the living room where he liked to punish us. I would lie there until I had the energy to stand up, looking around at the fussy little figurines of women in Victorian dresses that my mother liked to collect. They were her pride and joy. I used to fantasise about smashing every one of them. I hope Riley will know to be careful around them. The weird feeling I get whenever I think about my parents returns, the little metaphorical tap that there is something I am supposed to remember, but I dismiss it.

Riley is staring at me, his green eyes dark with hate, but I don't need to worry about that now. It will all change once we're together and he has understood the magnitude of the truth. She took my boy from me. She shouldn't have been allowed to do that.

'I just need to know you're going to be quiet because if you're not…' I pick up the knife from where I've left it, relieved that he hadn't thought to grab it. 'You want them to live through all of this, don't you?' I wave the knife, gesturing at Scotty and Sam.

He nods, crying again. 'You said… said you weren't going to hurt me. How can you be my mum if you want to hurt me? Mums don't hurt their kids.'

He is sobbing now and I feel a twinge of something, but I'm holding the knife and the mallet and there's no way he would let me touch him. Sometimes a mother needs to do what's best for her child, even if her child doesn't understand it at the time. I square my shoulders. From today, I am a mother again and I need to do what's best for him. I keep my voice stern so he understands. 'You can shout to your heart's content down here and no one will hear you, so I suggest you keep quiet. If I go up there and I hear you making a noise, I will come back down and kill Sam and Scotty. You don't want that, do you, Riley?' I say, raising my voice over the noise he is making.

He shakes his head vigorously and he wipes his face and sniffs, which is a disgusting sound.

'Okay, I'll throw some chips down the stairs so you have something to eat. The television works so just sit tight. This will all be over soon.' I wait for a smile from him in recognition of this kind gesture, but I am not rewarded with what I need.

'Are you going to kill me?' he asks, more curious than scared.

His voice holds a hint of disbelief because this doesn't feel real. It doesn't feel real to me either. I had the whole thing worked out in my head. I needed to be near him, to watch him, to make sure, but of course from the first time I saw him, I knew him, recognised him. I sent the gifts and they worked, I'm sure they worked because how could they not have? Then I was going to get him to come and spend some quiet time with me and I would explain.

'I sent you the gifts, you know, all of them.' I anticipate how his eyes will light up and this will suddenly become easier. I'll tell him that he can have a new Switch so we don't have to go back to his house. But he doesn't behave the way I want him to at all.

He looks at me and then he glances at Sam who is lying still on the floor. 'I don't want them,' he whispers. 'You're not my mum.'

I feel the urge to hit him again but I take deep breaths and repress it. I have so much to offer him. I have the love inside me for a child and I have my parents. They will do better as grandparents, I'm sure of it. I will give them the one thing they want and they will love me for it.

'I'm coming with you,' I imagined him saying, 'I don't ever want to see her again.' But this feels wrong now. It's not working out the way I thought it would. I didn't want to hurt Sam and I certainly don't want to hurt Scotty.

Riley is looking at me, his eyes rimmed in red, Scotty held tightly against his chest again. I realise I haven't answered his question about whether or not I'm going to kill him.

'No, Riley, why would you think I would kill you?' I say, shaking my head. I need to get it together. I have a child to take care of now.

He shrugs his shoulders and looks down at Sam.

'I know you won't believe me,' I say, 'but you think that Beverly is your mum and she's not. I am. I'm your mother, your real mother.'

I search his face for something, some acknowledgement of what I've said but he hugs Scotty closer and his lips turn down. He is shutting me out, shutting the truth out.

I need to leave because I can feel myself getting flustered and sometimes when I get flustered or angry, I lose control. I don't want that to happen. I will tell him everything when things have calmed down. He won't believe me but at the back of the basement I have a backpack filled with things from when he was a baby. I have the soft blue blanket he used to like to be wrapped in, the velvet rabbit he slept with, and pictures of his first days in the world. His little scrunched-up face, his tiny hands. I took so many pictures of him. It was love at first sight; it really was. I could never get enough of holding him and I hated that I had to share him. I hated that he couldn't just be with me all the time. I thought about running away, just disappearing with him one night and never returning, but I wasn't ready. I needed time to get used to taking care of him before I ran. I needed to get some money together and I needed time to adjust. So, I waited, and because I waited, I lost him. I lost him for seven years, but I've found him now. He's mine and he's staying with me.

I climb the basement stairs slowly and when I get to the top, I look down at him. He is watching me. His gaze is filled with mistrust and dislike.

'Remember,' I say, 'you need to be quiet and behave or I will hurt Sam and Scotty. Nod your head if you understand.'

He nods slowly, more tears appearing. I unlock the door and then close it behind me. On the outside of the door there is another lock. I hoped I wouldn't need it. I quickly grab a bag of chips from the pantry and throw them down the stairs, not looking to see where they land. I slide the outside lock into place and sink wearily down onto Sam's sofa in his living room. I don't know how I'm going to convince him. If Sam wakes up, I don't know what I'm going to do about that.

I thought I had a plan, but all I had was an idea and a wish. That's not the same thing as a plan, not at all.

CHAPTER TWENTY-SEVEN

Beverly

Beverly shows the two constables who have arrived at her door to the living room. They introduce themselves as Constable Rivers, an older policewoman, and Constable Riyad, a bearded policeman. 'Would you like to sit down?' she asks, indicating the battered leather sofa. She experiences a momentary twinge of embarrassment at the state of the sofa; it has a piece of black duct tape across the centre of one of the pillows where three-year-old Riley experimented with scissors he had somehow managed to get out of a high cupboard by climbing up onto a cabinet. He has been a climber since he could toddle, and she had regularly found him on top of the dining room table if she took her eyes off him for even a moment.

She bites down on her smile as she thinks about this. At the time she was devastated at her failure to keep him safe and at the ruining of the sofa that she could not afford to replace, but as the years have gone by, it has turned into an amusing anecdote she has shared with the few friends she has made at mothers' groups over the years. They keep in touch mostly on Facebook these days, but everyone had thought it was an indication of Riley's independent spirit when she posted about it. She wonders if this will also be a story she tells people in the future, something that was terrifying at the time, but can be regarded with wry humour when he's older, as she watches him graduate from high school or get married.

'So,' says Constable Riyad after she has gone through what happened again, answered the same questions twice, explained one more time, 'you say he's never done anything like this before?' His dark eyes are creased in concentration and she wonders if she has, somehow, made a mistake, let something slip.

She had not expected the arrival of the constables at her house so soon, but even though it felt like hours, when she checked her watch, she realised that only twelve minutes had passed between her call to emergency services and their arrival. She had imagined that she would be told she had to wait a few more hours before getting the police involved. Riley wasn't a baby and he could be hiding or angry and walking off his feelings. But police respond immediately to missing children. She knows that now.

'No, I told you – never.' Beverly bites down on her frustration at the repeated questions. They must have their reasons.

'I know it's hard to keep answering the same questions,' says Constable Rivers, 'but we take missing child cases very, very seriously.' She has short grey-brown hair and tired brown eyes.

Beverly understands that she will be the first person they look to for an explanation. First blame the mother and then... then she doesn't know what else is possible.

They have asked the question about Riley running off three times now.

'I understand,' she sighs, not wanting to appear difficult.

'And his father isn't in the picture,' Constable Rivers states. Beverly pushes the birth certificate across the coffee table, making it clear that this is the case. The constable looks down and nods.

'It was a one-night stand,' she tells them and then she looks down as if this embarrasses her.

'You must have been young.' Constable Riyad smiles.

She nods. 'Only ei— twenty, I mean eighteen,' she says knowing that she can't lie to the police about how old she was when she became a mother. They have looked at her driver's licence

'It must have been difficult to raise a baby alone,' Constable Rivers says and Beverly nods again.

'Being a single mother can feel impossible at times,' the constable says gently.

Beverly starts to agree and then she looks at the constable and realises what the woman is doing. 'I didn't hurt my son,' she says, gritting her teeth.

'No one is saying that,' Constable Riyad says, but Beverly knows they were leading her down that path. First, they would act as if they cared and try to get her to open up, and then, hopefully, she would confess.

'Look,' she says, needing to make it clear, 'I had Riley because... well, both my parents died and it felt—'

'And, of course, you lost your brother, didn't you?' the constable says sympathetically, and the judgement Beverly reads in the woman's face softens for a moment. She shivers, feeling naked despite her clothes. They know everything. If they know about James, how much else do they know?

Tears of grief and fear force her to run for a tissue. Obviously they would know about James.

'Could I get you some tea?' she asks after she has blown her nose.

Both constables nod and she leaves them, grateful for some time in the kitchen alone to compose herself. On the windowsill above the sink, she touches Riley's line of toy cars, pushing the tiny red Porsche back into line with all the others as she waits for the kettle to boil.

In the living room, she sets a cup in front of each of them before going back to the kitchen and returning with the milk and sugar. The constables take their time getting their tea to their liking while she sits in the blue recliner where her father used to sit and tries to slow her breathing so that she won't throw up. *Oh, Mum and Dad, I miss you so much.*

'I guess I wanted a family of my own even though I was so young,' she says now. And both constables gesture their understanding.

'Let's take it from the start,' says Constable Rivers and Beverly takes them through it again. She tells them all the places she thinks Riley could be, explaining that she has checked all of them.

'We have a couple of patrol cars out in the neighbourhood right now, knocking on doors and checking all the parks,' says Constable Rivers and Beverly flushes at how serious this has become, at what this means for her son and the possibility of him simply walking through the door right now. This is really happening to her, actually happening. Her child is really missing.

'I contacted the class mother,' Beverly says, thinking about the efficient woman named Brenda, 'and she's sending around a WhatsApp to everyone so that all the children are aware that they need to tell their parents if Riley somehow makes contact or if he turns up at one of their houses.'

'Good,' says Constable Rivers.

'And I called the mother of his best friend,' Beverly adds, so they know she's done everything she can think of to do. Ada had immediately dispatched her older sons to go out and help look for Riley: 'They're taking Benji with them in case he might know of somewhere to look. It's too far to walk to our house but you never know with boys, they can be stubborn little buggers. Jeremy and Gabe are on their skateboards and Benji is on his scooter. They think they're having an adventure but believe me, if Riley is anywhere around here, they'll find him,' Ada told her.

'But it's getting dark and cold,' Beverly had protested, not wanting to feel responsible for Ada's children being out at night.

'They'll live,' Ada said.

She sounded completely sure that Riley would soon be found and, after Beverly ended the call and while she waited for the police, she allowed herself to release some of the tension she was holding in her shoulders that was forcing a shooting pain into her head. Ada was an experienced mother and she hadn't even been fazed by Riley running off. 'I've dealt with that too many times to count. The little darlings pack their bags and say they're off and I give them a sandwich for the road. They always come back. Don't worry yourself too much. I've had the police out twice and they find them so quickly you don't even get to enjoy some peace and quiet before they're returned.'

Her certainty allowed Beverly to imagine Riley would be home soon, tired and still a bit angry. Cold but accepting of her ruling on the Switch. She would put him in her bed after a warm shower and let him have a hot chocolate after dinner, overflowing with marshmallows. The thought of his smile at the unexpected treat comforted her.

But Beverly is doubting Ada's words now that the police are here, now that she has answered their probing questions and seen the way they are looking at her.

'So, we need to send out an Amber Alert if we haven't located him soon,' says Constable Riyad. 'Can you give us some of the most recent photos?'

At the words 'Amber Alert', Beverly's stomach sinks. She wants them to reassure her that Riley will turn up, that little boys do this all the time, that everything will be fine, but that's not what's happening.

She scrolls through her phone with shaking hands, finding one with Riley at the science fair at school last month where he won third prize for his inexpertly and slightly wonkily constructed volcano. His grin is a mile wide because he'd never won anything before.

Another one is of him in his school uniform at the beginning of term. She likes to take one on the first day of each term, knowing that one day she will look back through these photos and watch him grow from a tiny kindergarten child to a giant high-school student. *What if they don't find him? What if he never comes home? Don't think like that. Don't think like that.*

Each time she shows a picture to Constable Riyad he nods and then taps the photo to send it to his phone so it can be sent on.

'He's a sweet-looking little boy,' says Constable Rivers.

'Do you have children?' asks Beverly.

'I have three girls, all grown up now. They were lovely at eight, less lovely at sixteen, but they have turned out nicely.'

Beverly smiles even as she has to swipe a tear from her cheek. She wants to talk about Riley this way, imagining him as a lanky teenager, some spots on his face and an appetite she can't keep up with. 'I need to explain something about my ex-boyfriend,' she says now. 'It may be nothing but—'

'It's always good to tell us everything. The more we know the more likely we are to find Riley,' says Constable Rivers.

She explains about Ethan, about the gifts that he has left for Riley in the mailbox.

'Was he violent?'

'No.'

'Did he threaten you or your son?'

'No.'

'Did he do anything to make you feel unsafe?'

'No… well, I thought the last gift was a bit much. It's very expensive.' As Beverly says these words, she understands they make her sound a little ridiculous. *So he left gifts, so what?* But it doesn't feel like that. The fact that the notes weren't signed felt… threatening. She hunts them out for the constables who study and photograph them.

'Do you have his number?' asks Constable Riyad and Beverly hands over her phone.

'He hasn't responded,' she explains.

'Sometimes it's best if the call comes from another number. Otherwise, I can call it in and get someone to see if they can locate him. Give me a moment,' he says and he stands up and heads towards the kitchen, murmuring into his phone. Beverly watches him walking up and down and wishes she had cleaned up the mess on the countertop where she splashed tomato juice and spilled a drop of olive oil.

The constable returns to the room and says, 'No answer from his phone but I've called it in and someone is trying to contact him. I see you've tried quite a few times to get in touch with him.' He returns her phone to her.

A tingling discomfort over the constable going through her phone takes over but she knows she has no choice. There's nothing on there she has to hide. Riley has been using her phone to play on since he was a toddler. She would never have stored anything on there that he could accidentally find.

She puts the phone on the coffee table in front of her, leaving it there so they can see she's not trying to hide it. 'Yes,' Beverly answers the constable as she winds her fingers together, 'I've tried contacting Ethan many times over the last few days, and I've texted and called while I was looking for Riley. He's just not answering me.'

'Is that usual behaviour for him?' asks Constable Rivers.

'No,' says Beverly and then she shakes her head, worrying about Ethan for one stray moment, 'it's not.' It is unlike Ethan to freeze her out. Over the months they have been dating, he has always been the first to call after an argument, no matter how big or small. He is not a fan of the silent treatment. It was the reason why he broke up with his last serious girlfriend. 'If something is wrong, I would rather discuss it,' he had explained when they were talking about past relationships. Going quiet was not like Ethan at all. It's one of the reasons she fell in love with him, something that made him different to other men she'd briefly dated.

'What do we do now?' she asks because she's made them tea and her own cup sits cooling in front of her. She would like to run around the neighbourhood looking for her son, but she can't leave because she's been told to stay. It's nearly 6.30 p.m. and she's not sure how long he's been missing. She looked out of the window at 4.30 p.m., but who knows how long he could have already been gone? The constables stare at their phones, responding to messages, the minutes ticking by, Beverly's anxiety mounting with each moment that passes.

Constable Riyad's phone buzzes in his hand, startling Beverly, but then she feels her heart lift because maybe it's a call to say they've found Riley. She wants to leap up and return to making dinner because he will be hungry when he gets home.

'Yeah okay, yeah, no worries,' he says and he gets up, walking out of the room, murmuring into the phone too quietly for her to hear the words. She brings her little finger to her mouth, absent-mindedly chewing on the nail until she sees Constable Rivers studying her and she hastily sits on her hands. *What are they talking about? Have they found him?* Constable Rivers takes a silent sip of her tea, her face composed, sympathy in her gaze. Beverly feels sick.

When Constable Riyad returns to the living room, he's not smiling.

'Beverly, that was a call from my sergeant,' he says, his dark eyes filled with concern, forcing her heart into her throat.

'What—' she begins.

'They've found Ethan.'

'Oh,' she says, thinking, *What a strange way to say that – as though he's dead.*

CHAPTER TWENTY-EIGHT
Riley

Riley has no idea what to do. He looks down at Sam. He's lying on the floor like he's asleep, but Riley knows he's not asleep. He gets off the sofa and crouches down next to Sam, placing his hand on his chest the way he'd seen someone do in a movie once. He holds his breath so he can really feel if Sam's chest is moving or not. Sam's chest moves up and down slowly, as though each breath is taking him a long time but at least it moves. He's breathing and Riley sits down next to him, relieved and terrified. He lifts up Sam's dry hand and holds it. He's never held Sam's hand before and he looks down at the black marks on it, like someone used a marker to make funny-shaped dots all over his skin. This must be what it feels like to hold a grandfather's hand. He doesn't have a grandfather or a grandmother. He's the only kid in his class without grandparents or a father and that doesn't feel fair. If he had a dad, he would rescue him, he's sure. He imagines a man with hair the same colour as his breaking down the basement door and shouting his name. His mum is not as big as the woman who locked him in here, so he's not sure she could rescue him.

Scotty trots over to him and sniffs at Sam, licks one of his cheeks.

'He's just sleeping,' Riley whispers to the little dog and Scotty curls up next to his owner, satisfied with this explanation.

'Why would she say Mum is not my mum?' Riley asks the little dog. 'How can she not be my mum? How can that woman be my mum?' The woman must be crazy or mad, or cuckoo, as Benji would say.

He is trapped in here with Sam and Scotty and he has no idea how he can get away and he's never met a crazy person before. The woman who locked him in here must be really crazy. Why would she have sent him presents? Now that he knows they were from her and not from his dad the spy, he feels sad. He hasn't told his mum, but he wishes for a dad every night and he thought his wish had come true because he had wished it so much. But it hasn't and his dad really is dead and that makes him even sadder than ever.

If he had known the Switch was from the mad woman, he would never have wanted to play it and then he and his mum wouldn't have had a fight and now he would probably be home eating dinner which he is sure is spaghetti. A growl from his stomach makes Scotty lift his head and cock it to the side a little. Riley stands up and goes to get the chips. He needs to think of a way to get out of here, but he can't come up with a plan, just a whole jumble of thoughts going nowhere. Sighing, he turns on the television and climbs onto the sofa. 'I'm too hungry to think,' he tells Scotty. Sometimes when he gets really cross his mum says, 'Riley, I think you may be hungry, have a muesli bar,' and even though he doesn't believe her, he has one and then everything feels kind of better. What if she's not really his mum? He shakes his head. *It's not possible, just not possible.* The chips are salt and vinegar flavour which is not Riley's favourite because the vinegar bit makes his lips sting, but he eats them anyway. At least the mad woman gave him some food. His mum would say that he needs a proper dinner before any junk food, but this woman is not like his mum. She's not like any mum he's ever met so she can't be his mum – it's not possible.

At school once they had a lecture from a policeman about talking to strangers. It was mostly to do with internet stuff, and it seemed like bad people were mostly men. There was a picture of a man in the shadows and the policeman said that sometimes terrible people pretend to be kids so that other kids will trust them. He never said anything about women being terrible though, or about a woman pretending to be your mum. The woman said she's Sam's carer, although that's probably not true. If she was his carer, she wouldn't have hurt him. She came to clean the art room at his school when Benji spilled the paint, and he and Benji saw her walking in the playground with her mop and bucket as well. He doesn't know how long she's worked at his school for because he wasn't really paying attention, but he knows he's seen her around. 'Are you paying attention, Riley?' his mum always asks when she's telling him how to do something and he always says he is, but sometimes other stuff is going through his head. Maybe other stuff has been going through his head whenever he sees the cleaner lady. He wishes now he'd paid more attention. Has she trapped him down here because she is really cross about the red paint? But then why did she call him a nice boy? That was a lie and if she was lying about that she's probably lying about his mum not being his mum.

'She's probably lying,' Riley says to the dog who is sitting at his feet, waiting politely for a chip. 'We have to figure something out, Scotty,' he says and he hands the little dog a chip and watches him crunch it up. 'We have to escape from here.'

Putting the bag of chips down next to him, he licks his fingers and stands up, looking around the basement room. He's never been down here. When he comes over to play chess with Sam, they always sit upstairs in the living room. Riley likes playing chess with Sam because he has a special little table that is actually a chessboard. 'Chess is a game of strategy and planning,' Sam always tells him. 'You always need to think a few moves ahead.'

'That's what we need to do, Scotty,' says Riley, and the dog's triangular black ears prick up as he raises his head from sniffing for chip crumbs. 'I need to think a few moves ahead.'

There is a window high up on the basement wall. It doesn't look like it's been opened for a long time. It's long and narrow and the glass is really dirty. Maybe, just maybe, he can fit through it. But it's really high up and there's not really anything to stand on.

As Riley is contemplating the window, Sam groans and moves his eyes opening and his hand going to his head where the mad woman hit him. The mad woman who he refuses to believe is his mum.

CHAPTER TWENTY-NINE

I'm not sure what to do now. *How soon before people come looking for him?* In the days I've been watching her, I noticed that she always calls him in for dinner at around five. It's nearly seven now so she'll know that he's been missing for nearly two hours. Has she already called the police or is she out looking for him?

I don't know how long I have before police come knocking and I need to convince him to come with me. If I can get him to come with me, we can go to my apartment, and they won't find us for… well, forever, if I'm careful.

I don't work at the school. But it's a relatively large school and there are lots of people walking around. If you carry a mop and bucket, no one questions what you're doing and if they had, well, running was always an option. I bought my own bucket and mop, just walked through the school carrying them as though I was on some sort of mission to get somewhere. I had to clean up a few disgusting things, but it was worth it to be in the school, walking around unnoticed. It was just luck that I was outside his class when one of the kids spilled the paint. Well, not luck. I had been lurking around his classrooms, pretending to be busy. His teacher gave me a really funny look when he saw me on Wednesday, but I dropped my head and shook my mop and he walked on. I am good at blending in, at seeming as though I have always been there – you just haven't noticed me.

In Sam's kitchen I open the fridge and grab some cheese, cutting off a piece to chew while I think. The only option is to take him out of here and then back to my apartment, my cramped little apartment, filled with boxes I haven't unpacked because I knew I wouldn't be staying long.

I need to keep him away from everyone else until he believes what I'm saying. Until he wants to be with me. I believe that a few weeks with me will convince him that I'm the one he should be with. Then maybe we can leave the country for a bit or… no, that's stupid, I don't have his passport. Maybe we can leave the state. I can dye his hair a different colour. I've heard of that happening.

I cut another piece of cheese, enjoying the sharp taste as ideas start crashing into each other inside my head. How will I get him to come with me?

I wish that I had someone to talk to about this. I experience a strange desire to call my parents but they won't want to hear from me. When I turn up with their grandson, they will be more receptive. That's what I need to do. I need to take him to my parents and then I'll get their help, I'm sure of it. We can live with my parents. We'll be one big happy family, three generations under one roof.

I take out my phone and look up their number, my thumb hovering over it, and then before I can stop myself, I press it, holding the phone to my ear with my heart beating fast, the cheese now gluggy in my throat.

'The number you have called is no longer in service. Please check the number before calling again.'

That's odd. For as long as I've been alive my parents have lived in the same house and have had the same home phone number. I don't have their mobile numbers because neither of them had mobile phones when I moved out and it wasn't like they were going to call me and give me their numbers. They were glad to see the back of me. I think back to a year ago when I went over to their house. Through the lighted windows I watched the two of them moving around the kitchen. They didn't seem to be talking to each other. But then they were never very big conversationalists. A year ago, they were there. *Where are they now?*

Did they know I was watching them? Did they sense it and leave? Moving to the sink, I fill a glass with water and drink deeply. Something stronger than water would be good right now but I need to keep a clear head. They've probably just changed their phone number. I'm sure they're still in the same house with the same stone wall that will be covered in sweet-smelling jasmine in spring.

I would like to call my sister and ask her if she knows what's going on but that's not possible. Even though we formed some kind of a connection as adults, that's long gone now. I'm on my own until I get him out of the house and show him to my parents. Everything will be fine after that.

CHAPTER THIRTY

Beverly

'Ethan has been in hospital for the last three days,' says Constable Riyad.

'What?' asks Beverly, feeling stupid and confused. 'What do you mean?'

'He's in hospital,' the constable says. 'He had an accident and he has a broken arm, which they've operated on, and a concussion.'

'But he… but he was texting me and calling me,' says Beverly, rubbing at her hair, wanting to pull at it in frustration. 'He was texting me.' When had she last received a text from Ethan? She picks up her phone and scrolls through Ethan's messages and sees that the last text was Monday night. The rest of the messages have been from her to him, unanswered. 'He hasn't actually texted me since Monday night.'

'I don't know exactly what time the accident was, but it was on Monday. You said the presents were hand-delivered so it couldn't have been him.'

'No… I suppose… a car accident?'

'Yes, a car accident,' says the constable.

Beverly groans and drops her head into her hands because she is a horrible person, a terrible person.

'Is he okay? I mean, he's going to get better, isn't he? Will he be okay?' She thinks of Ethan in pain in a hospital bed. If she had known she would have visited him, regardless of the break-up. I she had known, but she was too busy telling him to stop contacting her to think about why he hadn't responded to her texts and calls. She hates to think of him opening his phone and seeing all those messages from her.

'It sounds like he should be fine,' says the constable.

Guilt stabs at her. But she had no idea and she doesn't know why his sister wouldn't have called her. She doesn't have Fiona's number but she'll find it. With her gaze focused on her shoes, Beverly prays for his safety and for his recovery, her eyes hot with tears.

'Poor Ethan,' she moans.

She had been wrong about him. He had only ever wanted a conversation. He has not been sending Riley presents. She shoves her phone in her pocket. If he wasn't sending the presents, who was? Fear prickles up and down her arms. Who was sending the presents if it wasn't Ethan?

'I just need… some water,' she says to the constables, making sure to keep her voice steady. If Ethan had not been sending the gifts, then who had? The question circles in her head. Round and round. The question circles but refuses to land on the answer she is avoiding. It's not possible. She knows that. So who sent the gifts?

In the kitchen, instead of water Beverly pours herself a mouthful of wine and swallows it, the acidic tinge focusing her thoughts. Knowing she doesn't want to smell like alcohol, she pours some of the orange juice Riley likes, even though she hates orange juice, and drinks that.

Despite her best efforts, the past claws at her, reaching out and taking hold. One image after another assaults her. Her parents waving goodbye as they got into the car to go away on their trip. 'You behave now,' their mother had said, smiling, knowing she and James would only order pizza and watch movies. She sees James's smile, hears him laughing and then sees him the way he was in the weeks before his death. The terrible change that took him over, as his eyes sank into his head and the weight fell off him. He always looked like something was bothering him, troubling him, and even a fleeting smile disappeared quickly from his face. Beverly knew exactly what – or who – was bothering him. All her instincts about Georgia had been right, but she kept that thought to herself. She wishes she hadn't now, wishes she'd said more, done more.

She takes herself back to the night her brother revealed that Georgia was pregnant. 'What are you going to do?' she had asked him.

'I don't know,' James said. He had loped off to the kitchen and returned with another beer.

'A two-beer night,' she joked, remembering that her father always said that after a particularly stressful day at work. He was always happy to have one beer at the end of the day, but some days he needed more than one.

James had laughed but there was no real mirth in it.

'Are you going to marry her?' Beverly finally asked, her voice small with despair. She was going to lose her brother and her home; she could feel it and she wouldn't even be able to argue that she should stay. A family needed a home and James was going to be part of a family.

'She wants to; she wants a wedding, a family, the whole thing.'

'And what do you want?' Beverly had asked, sensing his hesitancy.

He had put the beer down and turned to look at her. 'I don't know,' he said. 'I thought I loved her but when I try to imagine spending the rest of my life with her, I just don't know. Sometimes I get the sense she's hiding parts of herself from me, that she's never telling me the whole truth about herself.'

'What would she have to hide?'

'No idea,' he sighed. 'Maybe her parents were worse than she's said, although they sound as horrible as people can get, but maybe… maybe there was more going on.'

Beverly shook her head. 'They beat her and they didn't want her. I don't know how much worse it could get.'

She had been busy with her final year of school and friends, and now she knows that she didn't notice the new wrinkles appearing on James's forehead. She did notice that he lost patience with her, that he delivered more lectures about chores and studying and boys. As the months of Georgia's pregnancy passed, he became more and more strident and argumentative.

'Oh my God,' she had shouted at him one night after he had yelled at her for not taking out the recycling, 'you sound like a five-hundred-year-old man, what is wrong with you?'

James had opened his mouth to yell back and then he had dropped onto the sofa in the living room where they were standing, burying his head in his hands. She could hear that he was crying, his shoulders began heaving and she hadn't known what to do. She had known that he had cried after their parents' death because sometimes it was obvious, but he had done it away from her.

'What's wrong, what's wrong?' she had said, panicked, sitting down next to him and touching him on his back, 'What's wrong?' she asked again more urgently, putting both arms around him and squeezing tightly.

'It's Georgia,' he said. 'I told her that I don't want to get married and that I don't feel we're right for each other.'

'You're very different people,' Beverly had said cautiously, not wanting to push her own opinion.

'Yeah, and I'm noticing it more and more. I told her that I would support her and the baby, that I will do whatever I can, but she's just… she's been behaving so strangely these past few months. She won't see a doctor or go for a scan or anything like that. She doesn't want anyone telling her what to do and now she wants to reconnect with her parents even though they were horrible and abusive. She calls me constantly, checking up on me and telling me I need to let her know wherever I am, whatever I am doing. She has all these strange ideas about raising a kid, about letting them cry, smacking them, and teaching them discipline. It's like she's become a totally different person. And now I'm worried about how she'll raise a child. I don't trust her anymore. I don't know what's wrong with her, it's like some switch has been thrown and she's not coping with life or something.'

'Wow,' had been all Beverly could say.

'What am I going to do, Bev?' James said. He had genuinely seemed to be asking her the question.

'I'm really sorry, James… I know that I don't like her, but I hate that you're so unhappy. I want you to be happy. I wish I knew how to help but… I mean, it's not like you can raise a child on your own and it's not like she's going to give you custody anyway. You'll have to go and see a lawyer, put some custody stuff in place so you get to see the baby. That's what I would do, if you can do it. And when the baby is here, I can help. It will be amazing to be an aunty and I love kids.' She had smiled, imagining a baby with James's brown eyes or maybe with green eyes like Georgia. 'I can help you take care of him or her, and I can teach him stuff, like how to climb that tree out the back where Dad built you the platform to sit in.'

'I'll teach him to climb the tree, Bev, you fell and broke your arm.'

'Maybe I can teach him to cook,' she laughed, and she was relieved to see him smile. 'It will be fine, we'll manage – you'll see. And maybe Georgia will be… a good mother?' Even as Beverly said the words, she knew he would hear that she didn't believe them.

'Maybe… I don't know,' he sighed, 'but if I have your help we can manage.'

She had put her arm around him again. 'We can manage,' she said.

Things had become worse after the baby was born. But Beverly had no idea how bad things could get. She feels a shudder run through her at the memory and she drinks some more juice before returning to the living room.

'You okay?' asks Constable Rivers and Beverly nods even though she is completely not okay, but what else can she say? She sits down on the sofa, smoothing her hair away from her face and tying it back with a hair tie she has around her wrist.

'Now, is there anyone else who could have sent the gifts?' Constable Rivers asks. 'Are you sure that there are no other family members who might have wanted to give Riley a present?'

Beverly would like to screech the word 'No' at the constable because she is entirely sick of this question. They've been here for a short time and they keep asking it in case she has somehow forgotten that she has other family. She knows how this works. She knows what they're trying to do because she wants to tell them, she is almost desperate to confess the truth. It's how they break people in interrogations in those little rooms at police stations. They just keep asking the same question over and over again until the person tells them what they want to hear.

She would like to tell them that he does have other family. That there are people who would want to send Riley presents for all the wrong reasons. She would like to say, 'There are others but they don't know about him. At least I hope they don't because if they do, they know he's not mine.'

'Sam,' yelps Riley and he rushes over to the old man.

'What the hell just happened?' asks Sam. 'Riley, what are you doing here? Who was that? Scotty, stop licking me, old boy.'

'Let me help you sit up,' says Riley because Sam's hands are shaking and his face is very white, except for the part where he got hit and that's a gross purple-black colour. 'Do you want some water, or I have some chips?' he says, not sure what to give an old person who has been hit on the head. His heart is racing but he is so relieved that Sam is awake and not dead. Sam is an adult and he'll know what to do.

'Help me, lad,' says Sam and Riley grabs the man's hands as he holds them out and pulls him up until he is sitting kind of straight with his back against the sofa.

'Your mum is looking for you,' says Sam, rubbing his head.

Riley chews on his lip, unsure if he should tell Sam what the woman said. Sam might decide that he's the mad one, but he didn't hit Sam and only a mad person would hurt an old man like Sam. 'That woman upstairs says Mum is not my mum.'

'What?' says Sam. 'That's… look we have to leave here. Help me up the stairs and I'll take you home.'

Sam seems like he's confused. He doesn't understand. 'We can't leave, Sam,' says Riley patiently, worrying now because if Sam is confused, how is he going to help them escape? 'That woman hi you on the head with a hammer thing and she's locked us in.' Riley's eyes burn and his nose starts to run because he's really worried now. He goes to the bathroom and grabs some toilet paper to blow his nose. He doesn't want Sam to think he's a baby but he's getting really scared. Who is going to help them if Sam can't?

When he comes back, Scotty is sitting on Sam's lap. 'Look, explain this all to me again, Riley,' says Sam, 'and start at the beginning. Who is that woman and how did I end up down here?'

Riley starts at the beginning as Sam listens and strokes Scotty's soft fur.

'Why would she say your mum is not your mum?' replies Sam. 'That's just ridiculous. I remember meeting you when you were a baby. Your mum brought you over to meet me and Marjorie, and Scotty of course.'

Riley nods as though he remembers it, grateful that Sam remembers him as a baby and that what the mad woman said is not true, not true at all.

'Funny,' says Sam, 'I've had the strangest feeling all week that someone was in the house. I thought it was Marjorie, you know… her spirit visiting me, but maybe this woman, the one who hit me, has been here all along.'

'I don't…' begins Riley, not knowing what to say to this. He liked Marjorie and was sad when she died. She used to make card towers with him, building them higher and higher until the smallest movement in the air made them collapse. She always laughed when that happened.

'Right,' says Sam, looking around the basement room, 'let's get us all out of here.' He pats his pockets. 'Bugger, I must have lost my phone or something, I don't have it. Your mum called me to ask where you were and I came straight home to see… No, it's not lost… I put it on the kitchen bench to charge and that's when I heard you, you were yelling.'

'I was,' says Riley, relieved that Sam is remembering stuff. 'You said when we were playing chess that it was all about planning and strategy. Maybe planning and strategy can help get us out of here?'

'Yes, true, true, but what does that have to do with us now?'

'I have a plan,' says Riley, 'or I think I do, but I need some help.' He smiles at Sam because this is beginning to feel like an adventure and he imagines himself in a movie or a television show. Maybe he doesn't have a dad who is a spy, but maybe he can pretend to be one. He's a spy trapped by a bad woman and he needs to escape.

Upstairs they hear a chair moving across the floor and Riley shakes his head. This is not an adventure. If the woman would hit Sam, imagine what she would do to him? They need to get out of here quickly.

'Right, son,' says Sam, 'tell me the plan.'

CHAPTER THIRTY-TWO

I stand with my ear up against the basement door. I can hear him and Sam talking and I'm relieved that Sam is okay. He's a nice old man and I'm a nice person. I didn't want to hurt him. I step away from the door and catch a glance of myself in the mirror that hangs on the wall. I smooth down my brown hair and push my fringe out of my eyes. A lot of men have found me pretty over the years. It's easy enough to meet a man, to go on a few dates, to start a relationship. But it's harder to make things last.

'There's something wrong with you,' a man once told me. 'You need to get yourself some help.' He thought I had become too clingy, too over the top, and too emotional. I wanted to get married and have children. I wanted to establish a family for myself, to create what I had never had. What I should have had. I saw myself as one of those perfect mothers at the school gates with my hair neatly tied back, laughing at something clever my child says. On every first date with a man, I would try to imagine him as a father, visualise what the mixing of our genes would produce, whose eyes and whose hair the child would get. I asked questions, lots of questions, about their families and their plans for the future. Most men didn't call after that, but some of them did. It didn't bother me. I only needed one man. One good man. And if I couldn't find him, if I couldn't convince one man that he loved me enough to marry me, I was prepared to allow myself to get pregnant and take my chances. A good man would marry me.

A good-enough man would help me raise the child; a bad man would leave, but either way I would have a baby at the end of it

Men are not easy to mould and control but children are. I've known for most of my life that a child would bring me the love I needed, the love I never got from anyone else.

Riley is that child. The only way I'm going to get him to come with me is if he can't fight me. The only way he won't be able to fight me is if he's asleep. I go to Sam's bathroom and open his cabinet searching for what I need. 'Yes,' I say, fizzing with joy, because right here is the solution. I don't know how much Valium would be too much for a child and he's going to be heavy to carry but it's the only way. I find some juice in Sam's fridge and I begin crushing up the pills. There are ten left in the packet. That should do it.

CHAPTER THIRTY-THREE

Beverly

Beverly sucks deeply on the stale cigarette, relishing the immediate head rush she gets. It's impossible to stare at the constables anymore as they wait for their calls to come in. Their phones keep ringing with more questions from the missing persons' division who have now gotten involved. One of the detectives will be here soon to interview her. Each time one of the constables' phone rings, her heart lifts because maybe they've found him, and then it sinks again from the quick shake of the head they give her. She is going mad.

Desperation had driven her to the box of cigarettes buried on the top shelf of her cupboard. It was something to do with her hands, something to concentrate on for a moment. Constable Rivers had watched her search it out.

'Is it okay if I get a cigarette?' she had asked. It had occurred to her that smoking a cigarette would be a reason to be outside for a few minutes, maybe even alone for a few minutes.

'Up to you,' the constable had shrugged and then she had followed her to her bedroom.

She is not being left alone for more than a few minutes at a time. It feels solicitous but at the same time she knows they are waiting for her to do or say something that tells them whether or not she is simply a mother with a missing child or if she is a mother with a lot to hide. And because she does have a lot to hide, her shoulders and neck are in spasm as she reminds herself to pay attention to every single thing she is saying.

Perhaps if she tells the truth, it will help, but perhaps it will only hurt. What to say is tormenting her. How much or how little can she reveal without losing her son forever? Does she need to reveal anything at all to help find him? Does the fact that he's not hers have anything to do with him being missing? It's possible that he decided to take a walk and then… then what? Nightmarish scenarios involving white vans and strange men keep flashing through her mind.

Beverly has not smoked a cigarette for seven years and ten months. Those years have passed in the blink of an eye as she has gone from teenage girl to working mother.

She is standing just outside the kitchen door on the concrete step that leads to the back garden on one side and the driveway on the other. Riley's tree has faded into the shadows of the evening; the chill in the air makes her shiver.

She cannot help returning to the last time she had a cigarette – to that night seven years and ten months ago.

It was spring then, late – after 8 p.m. Some of the spring warmth was still hanging in the air, promising that a scorching summer was nearly there. She had been dropped home by a sympathetic policewoman. 'Someone from victim services will be in touch with you,' the woman had said. She can't summon her face, no matter how hard she tries, but she has a sense of a deep voice – scratchy like the woman was also a smoker.

Beverly had nodded her head and climbed out of the car and said, 'Thank you,' because her parents had always taught her to say 'please' and 'thank you', to show kindness and respect to everyone. Her parents thought that was how you lived a good and worthy life. She had intuited from them that living a life like that could somehow keep you safe from harm. She knew it wouldn't; it couldn't.

Slowly she had walked up the pebble pathway to her timber front door as she felt a moment of resentment towards the single-storey house painted white with green guttering. It had been a place of love and security, a place where she had always felt that the world was generally good, filled with good people all doing their best to live worthy lives. The death of her parents had been a terrible tragedy, but it had been an accident. No one sets out to kill someone, to actually take a life – or so she thought.

As she looked at the faded walls that were in need of a new coat of paint, she hated her home for a moment. The house had been a lie. Everything she had learned, everything she had been taught about the goodness of people, was wrong. People were capable of the most terrible things.

She was dressed in hospital scrubs. They had taken all her clothes to analyse the blood samples, to see if there was some tiny genetic clue to indicate that she was not telling the truth.

'It wasn't me, it was Georgia, Georgia – his ex-girlfriend,' she repeated to whoever would listen in the hospital. 'He was my brother, my brother,' she couldn't seem to stop telling people, as though this would make them understand the magnitude of her loss.

Her feet stopped moving at the front door; her keys, clutched in her hand, felt too heavy to lift. She turned and looked at the street and on seeing the police car still there, the constable inside waiting patiently for her to disappear from sight, she forced herself to open the door and go inside. The faint smell of turpentine mixed with the musky perfume she had used liberally that morning floated in the air. Her stomach turned over and she swallowed quickly.

An image of his body on the stained grey carpet, hours earlier, assaulted her, making her want to vomit. He had been wearing a black T-shirt because he always wore black T-shirts and when she had touched him, when she had returned to the apartment and seen him, had crouched down next to his prone body, grabbing and shaking him, the T-shirt had felt wet. Only when she had taken her hand away and seen it painted red had she realised. If she had been paying attention, she would have known with just a look. His eyes were darkened to almost black and his pupils were dilated, staring at nothing. But she shook him anyway, hoping that the cut on his neck was not that deep, despite the blood everywhere. Just everywhere. She had screamed for help. She remembered that: screaming for help but no one coming, as though people screaming for help in that particular apartment building was a regular occurrence.

In her house that used to be a home she left the lights off, preferring the dim light from the street. She reached for something to shake the image of her dead brother away, dragged an old bottle of whisky out of the liquor cabinet, swallowed two dusty gulps, coughing at the acidic chaser. And then she found her packet of cigarettes and lit one, taking so long she almost flung it away because her hand was shaking so much. She sank onto the sofa shocked into numbness. *Please don't smoke inside, Bev. Careful where you drop your ash, Bev. You really should give up smoking, you know.* His words, but he was not there to say them. He never would be again.

She was completely and utterly alone in the world. Her whole family was gone, and because they had never been very big to begin with, there was now just her, one eighteen-year-old girl to represent generations of the Cochran family; one pathetic eighteen-year-old girl.

If she had stayed when he asked her to leave, if she had insisted on being there when he talked to Georgia, if she had refused to listen to him, he might be alive. *If, if, if.* She might be dead but right now that seemed preferable. She could not imagine a reason to go on living weighed down by so much pain and so much loss.

They had given her some pamphlets at the hospital, tucked them into her hands as she left, but she thinks she may have dropped them on the floor of the passenger seat in the police car. She imagined the kind policewoman finding them and worrying that she did not have any information on how to deal with her grief, on how to go on living in a world that she no longer wanted to be in. But no pamphlet could help her understand why, after losing her parents, her brother was taken from her as well. She had never liked Georgia, but she had never imagined her capable of such a thing, never.

She finished the first cigarette quickly and then lit another, taking one more sip of the whisky, despite hating the taste. She went back over the day, unable to stop the memory taunting her.

Beverly wanted to take a shower, to get out of the hospital scrubs, but instead she remained on the sofa, whisky in her one hand and a cigarette in another, the hideous day clawing at her as she tried to make sense of it.

The baby was nearly two months old by this point. The relationship between James and Georgia was toxic with blame and threats being hurled back and forth. They couldn't even agree on a name for the baby, calling him simply, 'the baby'. The night he was born they had seemed blissful and almost in love again, but after a week Georgia insisted on taking him to the apartment that James was paying for, insisted on being alone with him.

Two months before the baby was born, Georgia told James her small apartment in a building without a lift was not the place she would be raising her child. She insisted on moving in with him and Beverly and when James said 'no', the relationship was finally over. Georgia threatened to take the baby out of state and James begged her to stay in Sydney, telling her he would find her a bigger apartment in the city and pay the rent. Each month was a struggle for him as he had to come up with more and more money, but he never complained. All that mattered was that his child had a safe place to stay and that he would be able to watch him or her grow up. But nothing was ever enough for Georgia. She knew the hold she had over James and she used it to get whatever she wanted from new furniture to things for the baby from expensive stores, to promises that he would be there whenever she needed him. James wanted her to stay with them until the baby was a little bigger and easier to care for, but Georgia told him she needed her space and Beverly could see the hint of a smile on her face as she said the words, 'You're the one who wanted us in a separate apartment James. But I'm sure you'll come whenever I need you.'

James had nodded. 'You know I will,' he said, and Georgia's smile grew wider.

They had argued every time James went over to visit, even as Georgia struggled to take care of the baby. 'She keeps telling me this wasn't how she thought it was going to be,' James reported to Beverly. 'She's saying stuff about him being difficult on purpose about him crying just to irritate her. Who thinks like that?'

Beverly didn't have an answer for her brother. She felt a sliver of fear for her nephew, troubled by the words Georgia was using. She adored the baby and hated the idea that his mother was saying such strange things.

'He's my child too,' she heard James say in every phone conversation with Georgia. 'I get a say in how he's raised. Don't let him cry. He's just a baby. Let me have him for a week. You can rest. No Georgia, I'm not trying to steal him from you. Please listen to me.'

He would pace the house, his voice rising and falling as he argued with his former girlfriend. Beverly stayed out of his way, cooked dinner for herself and just hoped that the two of them could reach some kind of compromise.

'I feel like she's got someone else in her life,' James told her. 'She keeps telling me that she doesn't want me in the baby's life, that she has enough help to raise him, but when I ask her about it, she won't tell me who it is. I don't want my child to call another man "Dad".'

'No way that's going to happen,' Beverly said vehemently, anger flaring. 'We won't let that happen.'

Georgia became irrational, accusing James of wanting to steal the baby away from her every time he visited. She was always suspicious when James came over, refusing to leave him alone with the child. She was sleep-deprived and refused to sleep when the baby slept. 'A good mother stays awake,' she told James.

'I think she has some kind of depression,' James told Beverly. 'I don't know how to help her or what to do.'

'Maybe get her to let you take care of the baby for a few days? Maybe all she needs is some rest and she'll calm down,' Beverly suggested. She wanted the baby in their house with them, away from his increasingly irrational mother. She felt guilty sometimes that she didn't have more sympathy for Georgia who was obviously struggling, but she was refusing all the help James offered. Beverly had even texted her and suggested she babysit, only to be told: *You know nothing about taking care of a child. You and your brother need to back off!*

'I keep saying I should have the baby for a few days, but I have a feeling I'm going to have to get him away from her and call in some help from a doctor or something. I've got an appointment with Dr Barry next week. He'll help, I know he will.'

Sucking deeply on another cigarette that fateful night all those years ago, Beverly dropped her head into her hands as she had this thought. He never got to see Dr Barry. The appointment was four days away.

And then, like the sun coming out from behind a grey cloud, suddenly shining a bright light on everything, she realised that even as she thought endlessly about the baby, she had no idea where the baby was, no idea at all.

'The baby,' she gasped. 'Oh my God – the baby!' Guilt and fear and shame over her momentary forgetting swirled through her body.

Hours earlier, when she went to the apartment where Georgia and the baby lived and where James was babysitting for the afternoon, the baby hadn't been there, so where was he?

James had said… *What had James said?* Beverly's mind threw up images of her nephew with his wide smile and beautiful eyes. How could she have been thinking about him all this time but not known where he was? It was because James said… James had said he was safe. Beverly stood up and sat down again. Ash from her cigarette dropped onto the carpet and she pushed her foot over it, not caring about the grey stripe she created on the peach-coloured carpet. He had said that the baby was safe. *Safe where? Safe how?*

She sucked deeply on the cigarette again, finished it as her mind whirled.

What had he meant? 'Think, Beverly,' she commanded herself as she went over the afternoon. Another sip of whisky, another cigarette, even though her stomach was already queasy. The act of drinking and of lighting up was concentrating her mind, allowing her to focus.

That morning, the morning that began as all mornings did James had gone over to Georgia's apartment to babysit his child. 'Good luck,' Beverly had told him ruefully, knowing how difficult it was. He was excited to be allowed to spend time with his son. Georgia doled out visitation in minuscule amounts, keeping him from the baby for whatever reason she could think of:

'He has a cold.' … 'He didn't sleep well.' … 'He hasn't taken his whole bottle.' … 'It's too hot.' … 'It's too cold.' … 'I don't feel well.'

On days James was allowed to see the baby he had always prepared himself by dressing nicely, making sure his nails were short and clean. Georgia had hated that he was a plumber, wrinkled her nose when he discussed his work.

'What time are you home today?' he had asked Beverly before he left.

'I have work until two and then I'll be home,' she'd said. It was late October, her favourite time of the year, when all the gardens in the neighbourhood were a riot of colour with spring flowers in full bloom.

Beverly had finished her final exams and was saving up to travel around Europe in December, relishing the idea of snow and ice while Australia sweltered through summer. She had some inheritance from her parents but she wanted to keep her little nest egg so she could go to university and not worry about money. James had a child to support and she didn't think it was fair for him to keep supporting her after she left school. She had a job in a clothing store for older women five mornings a week and while she had taken what she could get at the time, it surprised her how much she enjoyed it.

The hours that day had passed peacefully. James had texted when she was on a break: *She seems in a good mood today* ☺

Beverly was happy for her brother and glad she got to see the message before her battery ran out. Her phone was old and never lasted more than a few hours. If Georgia was in a good mood, it meant James would be able to spend more time with his little boy.

Work had run later than she thought it would because she got involved helping a woman choose a dress for her granddaughter's wedding. 'You can go,' her boss, Louisa, told her, but she wanted to see the sale through.

On impulse she'd decided to stop off at Georgia's apartment before going home, hoping the woman had left James alone with the baby but knowing that if she hadn't, things would still be easier for James if she was there for a while. Georgia hated Beverly, but she still tried to control herself in front of her. Beverly hadn't seen much of the baby and when Georgia was there, she was never allowed to touch the child. She longed to see her nephew, adored holding him in her arms, rocking him and watching his eyes blink slowly as he drifted off to sleep. He was so light, so small, and yet he was such a little person already. If she got to hold him and talk to him, his tiny forehead would wrinkle slightly as though he was really considering what she was saying. It surprised Beverly how much she loved the baby, how much she wanted to cuddle him. If by some chance, Georgia was out, she might even get some time to hold him. After parking her car, she walked quickly to where the apartment was, knowing that she would never get enough time with him and wanting to get there sooner.

Georgia lived in a tall red-brick building that was still waiting for gentrification. It was slightly rundown but secure, and the shabby laminate kitchen and old carpeting in the apartment meant James could afford to cover the rent for Georgia and his son. Georgia complained about it constantly, hating the cooking smells that drifted through old air vents and the noise she could hear through the thin walls. Each time Georgia told James how unhappy she was, Beverly worried about the woman moving in with them. She would have loved to have her nephew close by and she knew that James wanted to live with his son, but Georgia was part of that and James knew that he couldn't live with Georgia. Her mood swings had him walking on eggshells most of the time. One minute she loved him and her son and the next she cursed them both for ruining her life. She threatened to take the baby and just disappear, hinting, 'You're not the only one I can get help from, you know.' James was talking to a lawyer, readying himself for a challenge in court because he knew it was coming. He could see a future where he would have to fight for visitation rights with his son. While the baby was so young, he was biding his time and trying to keep Georgia happy. It was all he could do.

James was surprised to see her at the apartment when she turned up.

'Why are you here?' he said when he opened the door, a worried look on his face. 'Why didn't you answer your phone? I've been calling you and texting you!' His voice rose as he spoke, his eyes darting from side to side, panic evident. 'You shouldn't be here; you said your shift ended at two. Just go home. You can't be here now.' He ran his hands through his hair, rubbed at his forehead.

'The battery went flat again, jeez. Anyway, I'm here now. I just came from work. I wanted to say hello to my nephew. Is she here?' she whispered.

'No… no, but Bev, you need to go home. The baby isn't here either.' His voice was still high with panic and she didn't understand why he was behaving so strangely.

'What do you mean? Where is he and why are you here if he's not? Where's Georgia?' She felt her eyes narrow as she questioned him. What was he hiding?

'I managed to get her to go out, to go to the hairdresser. I booked an appointment for her and I… look, you need to go home right now. The baby is safe. I have to tell her she needs help: I want her to get help. I'm going to ask her to let me keep the baby for a few days until I can get her some help. But I had to make sure that he was… I found a bruise on his back when I arrived today, like… I don't know. How does a baby get a bruise?'

'What do you mean, a bruise?' she asked, shock making her cold. The baby wasn't even rolling over yet. *How could he have hurt himself?* Beverly lifted her hand to her mouth. 'A bruise,' she whispered, horrified.

'A bruise, Bev,' he said, his own horror evident. 'All over his back, like someone hit him. It's faded to yellow, but it must have been… I can't believe it. She never told me about it. Why?'

'That's—' she began, revulsion at the idea of Georgia hurting the tiny baby making her feel sick.

'I'm not going to let her take care of him until she gets help.' He was pacing around Georgia's small apartment as he spoke, wearing a patch on the old grey carpeting, where stains from former tenants had never been fully removed. To Beverly he seemed scared but she wasn't sure if he was scared for the baby or actually scared of Georgia.

'That's… hideous. You can't let her have him then,' she said firmly.

'I know.' He stopped walking, faced her with a wild look on his face. 'You need to go home. I need to sort this out and you need to go home right now.'

'Stop shouting at me, James. I understand you're upset but none of this is—'

'Oh God,' he said, covering his face with his hands and taking a deep breath. 'I'm sorry, Bev, okay? Please, please just go home now. You can't be here. I'll be there soon.'

'But where is—'

The doorbell rang, startling them both. 'That's her,' he said. 'I told her not to take her keys in case I took him for a walk but… shit, she's back early. You can't be here. You just can't. Go home, I'll buzz her in, but she'll be up here quickly, just go home!' She had never seen her brother afraid of anything but he was obviously afraid of Georgia's reaction.

'No. Let me stay. I'll help you convince her to get help. Maybe she'll listen if I'm here.'

'Just go, just get out and use the stairs,' he yelled, his voice strained.

Shock at his desperate behaviour made her comply. James rarely yelled and yet he had shouted at her more than once in the last few minutes.

She held up her hands as she moved towards the door of the apartment. 'I'll wait at the park for you; I'll wait in case thing get difficult. I'll give you half an hour. My phone is dead, but I'll wait for thirty minutes and then I'm coming up.'

'No, go home. I said you need to go home,' he shouted, waving his hands at her.

'I'm starting the countdown now,' she called back as she flung open the door and ran for the stairs, hearing him tell her to go home again and again. James was so panicked and now that panic was coursing through her veins. How much worse had things become with Georgia? Was she actually hurting her own child, harming a small baby?

She waited in the park across the way from the building, sitting on a timber bench, weathered grey with age. For five minutes, ten minutes, twelve minutes, just watching the hands on her wristwatch go round and round, the spring heat warming her back. She looked up, forcing herself to look away from her wrist where the hands of her watch seemed to be moving backwards, and watched a little girl bounce a red ball as she counted. The park was filled with people walking in the sunshine. An old couple strolled past and smiled and nodded at her as her gaze strayed back to the watch face, anxiety mounting.

After fifteen minutes she got edgy, so she stood up and began walking across the street. She would ring the bell and get him to leave. If the baby was safe then fine, it could all be discussed tomorrow. But who would have the baby? A babysitter? A neighbour? No one James knew had children. James didn't even see his old friends anymore, not since Georgia became part of his life. But he'd said the baby was safe so he must be with someone. She would have babysat herself if he'd asked her to cancel work, but he hadn't. She had no idea why.

As she started to cross the street to Georgia's building, she watched the sliding doors open. Georgia dashed out, her hand clutching one of the baby's blue onesies. Her distress was obvious, her hair all over the place, not like she'd been to the hairdresser at all. She ran towards the traffic light and even from across the street Beverly heard her yell, 'My baby, my baby.' As she scooted past people, they stepped back quickly, needing to get away from her.

Beverly opened her mouth to call to her but thought it better to leave it. She was really upset, that much was obvious. Georgia must have been angry with him, must have refused to get help.

Thank goodness that James had left the baby somewhere safe – he was doing the best he could for his child. The image of the baby with a bruise on his back frightened her. She watched Georgia cross the street and disappear from view. She looked like she needed help, but Beverly needed to speak to James first, to find out what had happened.

Another resident had been walking into the apartment block and she had walked behind him, standing quietly while she waited for the lift, and all that time, all that time, her brother had been bleeding to death on the floor of Georgia's apartment, the door slightly open. All thoughts of the baby had disappeared as Beverly had screamed for help and then called an ambulance while trying to inexpertly keep his heart pumping. No one had heard him shouting although he must have shouted. He must have. She had only been in the park for fifteen minutes. It must have happened very quickly. Beverly had tried to imagine how Georgia would have grabbed a knife from the kitchen. Did she think James had stolen the baby from her? Had she listened to him at all as he explained she needed help? Had she simply attacked him on seeing him? There were too many questions and absolutely no answers.

Only later, back home on the sofa, clutching her whisky and cigarette, did she remember the baby, who was supposed to be safe.

Her phone was in her bag and she pulled it out, struggled to her feet and squished her cigarette in the ashtray. How would she find her nephew? Who had him? Perhaps there was a message on her phone, a number and a name – something to tell her where the baby was. It was so late. Any babysitter would be calling to ask where James was. The police had James's phone. Would they keep it on?

The first thing she needed to do was charge her phone. Walking with lead-filled feet she went to the kitchen and plugged in the charger that sat there. The screen remained blank, black, dead. It would need a few minutes.

Why didn't you tell me where the baby was? What were you thinking? How can you not be here to answer my questions? How is it possible that you are not here and never will be again? She stared at the screen of her phone, willing it to light up, needing it to be available to her so she could call… who? She had no idea who she was going to call or what she was going to say. A flash of anger made her grit her teeth. He should have told her where the baby was, but then he would have expected to be home by now, not lying in a morgue. She saw him in her mind then, naked, exposed, the large cut at the side of his neck stitched, raised and bloodied; her imagination was horrifying but not more horrifying that what had happened. She gave in to a river of tears as she tried to erase the image of her brother's body from her mind, sinking to the floor in the kitchen. How could he be dead? He had looked after her and he had tried to look after Georgia. He loved being a father and he had so many plans for his son. He was going to teach him to play cricket and he was going to take him to rugby games. He wanted to go camping and he had told Beverly that he would encourage him to go to university. The baby had felt like a new start for both of them, an extension of their little family that had suffered so much. *Where was the baby? Where could he be?*

Beverly's tears dampened the front of her hospital scrubs, her nose ran and a pain settled across her heart. How could James be gone – her beautiful brother who was good and kind? How could he be gone?

As she sucks at the stale cigarette now, Beverly cannot help th
tears that arrive at the memories of that terrible day. She recall
herself slumped on the kitchen floor in the dark, completely alon
in her terrible grief. She swipes at her face as she takes anothe
drag of the musty cigarette. She's going to get her son back. Thi
is not going to end with her alone again. There is no dissolvin
into grief when you're a mother. A mother needs to be strong
A deep breath calms her. Taking another drag of the cigarett
she imagines Riley wrinkling up his nose at the smell. He think
smokers are strange. He's never seen her smoke, but once, in th
courtyard of a shopping centre, he had pulled her sleeve. 'Loo
what he's doing,' he had said, shocked at the man sending plume
of smoke into the air from his nose.

Has her little boy run away? Has he been taken? Who woul
take him? Her mind scrambles for answers. Who else had h
mentioned? She drops the cigarette and turns, walking back int
the house.

'Mr Benton,' she says.

'Sorry?' says Constable Riyad, rubbing at his beard.

'Mr Benton is a new teacher and he's been asking all sorts c
questions about Riley's dad, like more than once. He asked hir
why he didn't see him and where his dad was buried and how lon
his mum and dad had dated. I thought it was weird. I was goin
to contact the school tomorrow. I was going to do it tomorrow.

'Okay,' nods the constable, 'we can contact the school. Hav
you met Mr Benton before?'

'No… he's new. He's a new teacher. But he went home early toda
that's what Riley said, he went home early. I don't know anythin
about him, nothing. He could be… anyone.' Her voice rises in pani

The constables exchange a quick glance and then Constabl
Rivers makes a call to the station. Beverly walks away, needin
another cigarette, needing something. *Who could Mr Benton b
What could he have wanted with Riley?*

CHAPTER THIRTY-FOUR

unlock the basement door. It's awkward because I have two glasses
of juice in my hands and the knife tucked into my jeans. I have
left the mallet upstairs because I can't carry everything.

The light in the basement is dim, the bulb in the lightshade
is dusty and there is a smell that I don't really like, a cooped-up
smell – there was only the slightly mildewed smell of books and
papers slowly fading with time when I first slept here. I wish that
window could be opened, although it's probably best if it isn't. I
tried a couple of times but it feels very stuck.

They both watch me walk slowly down the stairs. Sam looks
terrible, bewildered by what has happened, pale, with half his face
puffy and black. Riley clenches his fists, trying to look threatening
but he's just a small boy. His skinny legs are long in his shorts, his
knees knobbly. He's just a little boy. *My little boy*.

Scotty is asleep on the couch, unconcerned because he's with
Sam, and a lovely thought comes to me that one day very soon,
my son will sleep near me as well, happy to know he is safe with
his mother.

'I brought you both some juice,' I say brightly. I have mixed a
couple of Valium into Sam's juice too, just to give me some time
to leave in peace. Will a couple of Valium kill an old man? I think
not, but at this point I don't really care.

I place the juice on the old coffee table as they watch my every
move. They are standing close to each other and, as one, they look
hopefully at the stairs.

'Don't even try,' I say. 'Now, both of you, drink up.' I take th
knife out and wave it around a little, just so I don't need to forc
them. Neither of them picks up a glass. Gritting my teeth an
swallowing a sigh, I point the knife at Scotty. 'Please don't mak
me hurt him,' I whisper sadly as though it would hurt me t
hurt the little dog. I gesture at the glasses on the coffee table. Th
quicker they are both asleep, the sooner I can get away. Once he
asleep, I'll call a cab. It's easy enough to explain away a sleepin
child, any mother knows that. I could take Sam's car. It would b
easier but I'm not sure how long he'll be asleep for and a car ca
be traced by the police.

'I don't want juice,' says Riley, defiant, lacing his hands togethe
behind his back like a much younger child would do. I can see th
motherhood is not going to be as easy as I thought it would b
I knew that babies were difficult. Riley was an especially difficu
baby who hated sleeping. But I did think it would be easy nov
Once I got over the shock of seeing that he was alive and well,
imagined an easy reunion and peaceful days. But he's obviousl
been raised badly.

'Drink it now,' I threaten quietly and I look meaningfully a
Scotty, the knife upright in my hand. They glance at each othe
and then Sam sighs.

'Look, love,' he says softly. 'I don't know why you're here c
what you hope to achieve but you have to let us go. I tell you wha
why not just leave and then Riley and I will cook up a story abou
me falling down the stairs? This can all be over right now and n
one ever has to know the truth.'

'I don't think so,' I reply. 'I came for my son. He's my son.'

Sam looks from Riley to me and then down at Scotty. He
trying to find the words that will work, but no words will convinc
me to leave. I've come this far. I'm not leaving without my chil

'If Riley comes with me now in your car, then I will leave.
need you to come with me, Riley, and we can go somewhere sa

and I can prove to you that I'm your mother. Tell him, Sam,' I say, keeping my voice soft and the knife lowered. 'Tell him to come with me and I'll go. All you need to know is that I'm his mother and he needs to be with me.' I am calm and logical, and Sam appears to be listening, Riley too: his eyes widen and his mouth drops open a little, his terror obvious, but there's nothing to help that right now. I would rather he fear me than that he tries to defy me. A good mother needs to have her child's respect.

'Well,' says Sam, spreading his arms wide, 'I for one believe you.'

'Please don't make me go with her, Sam,' cries Riley, clutching at the old man's shirt.

Sam puts his arm around him. 'Now wait a minute, Riley. I've told this young lady that I believe her and we need to discuss this. What's your name?'

'Oh, never mind that. You said you believe me. Do you? Do you really?' I ask, delight in my heart. It's such a relief to finally have the truth acknowledged after all these years. I put the knife down on a little round table next to me. I want to hug Sam. I step towards him, but he and Riley take a small step back, uncertainty on their faces.

'I do,' he nods and smiles, holding up a hand to keep me back, 'but perhaps you've gone about things the wrong way. Why don't we call in the police and you can explain it to them and then if they're fine with it, of course Riley will come with you.'

Burning fury surges through me and I grab the knife and hold it towards Sam's face. 'Don't you dare try and manipulate me, old man. I'm not an idiot.' I gesture with the knife and then I look at Scotty.

'Don't, please,' begs Riley.

'Now just a minute,' says Sam, his hand up again.

The doorbell rings and all three of us look up.

'That'll be the police,' says Sam, his relief obvious. 'Bev will have called them.'

I flinch slightly, panic rippling through me. But then I realis
that they are simply going from house to house. They must b
doing that, checking the whole neighbourhood. They have n
idea I'm here. There is no way Beverly would suspect it's me, n
way at all. I knew it was only a matter of time before she calle
the police.

I could just ignore it but Sam's car is in the driveway.

'When I come back, the juice needs to be gone,' I say, 'or there'
be trouble.' I wave the knife at Scotty. I smile as I walk up th
stairs. I remember my mother saying, 'There'll be trouble,' and
knew that if I didn't do what she said I would suffer for it. I fee
like a real mother, making sure her son does what he's told. It
what's best for him, after all.

I paint a smile on my face, an excuse ready.

There are two policemen at the door, both overweight an
far too old to be doing this. They are wearing jackets and I'r
surprised by the chill. I hate the cold. Perhaps my son and I ca
move to Queensland where it's always warm. Maybe my paren
can come with us. They can buy a house for us all to live in. S
many wonderful thoughts are filling my head that it's hard to kee
track of them all. I offer the policemen a bright smile.

'We're looking for a missing child,' one of them explains an
he shows me a picture of Riley on his phone.

'Oh, he looks so sweet,' I reply. 'When did he go missing?'

'Today. Isn't this the residence of Samuel Waters?' he ask
looking down at his phone where I can see a list of people's name

'Oh yes, but Sam's in Melbourne visiting his daughter Liza
I'm dog-sitting. I haven't seen the child, but I could come an
help you look. That poor mother must be out of her mind wit
worry.' My voice is dripping with honey, my concern genuin
All I want to do is help.

The policeman gives me a long look and I understand I hav
overdone it slightly.

'I haven't seen him but I will keep a lookout,' I say, emphasising the words to let them know that I definitely will.

They both nod. 'Thanks, please call us if you do see him.' One of them turns back and hands me a card and they amble off to the next house.

I need to wait a while for the Valium to kick in. They'll drink the juice, I'm certain of it.

Exhausted, tired, I sit down in the kitchen with a bottle of Sam's red wine and pour myself a decent glass. The sooner I am in the cab on the way to my parents' house the better. I think about how they looked the night I went over to see them a year ago, the night I watched them from the garden, accepting the cold so that I could stand there. I saw that their old gas heater was on in the living room, the orange flames flickering merrily. They'd had it for decades and I was surprised it still worked and that they had never worried about gas leaks. They both looked older, but I knew they would. I was glad they were both still alive, but I didn't approach the front door to ring the bell. I had nothing to offer them then. I will have something now.

My parents love their house. My father is out in the garden every Sunday and fixes things inside as soon as they break. My mother likes everything to be very, very neat. My sister and I got a good smack if things in our bedrooms were messy. I have to say it has made me a very tidy adult. I prefer things tidy. I hope Riley does as well.

I have a vision of the four of us in the garden, enjoying lunch in the sunshine under the gazebo. I can see my parents' faces, my mother touching her grey curls to pat them back into place and my father smiling as he runs a handkerchief over his head because he sweats in the heat. I see them both look over at me and smile and say, 'Thank you for finally giving us the son we've always wanted.'

I finish my glass of wine, holding on to the lovely vision. I can't wait for it to come true.

CHAPTER THIRTY-FIVE

Riley

'One more shove, Riley, go on, help me,' says Sam and Riley pushes hard, feeling his arms hurt. The desk is heavy because it's covered in stuff and they don't have time to take it all off. The mad woman will be back at any minute.

'Right, I think that's as close as we're going to get,' says Sam. 'Hop on.'

Riley clambers onto the desk, finding what little space he can to put his feet. He reaches up his arms. 'I can push it, Sam. I'm high enough now.'

'Well, give it a good shove, lad. I don't know when it was last opened.'

It's not warm in the room but as Riley pushes and pushes against the timber frame of the window he begins to sweat. His heart is racing as he pushes with all his strength. If she comes back and finds them doing this, they're in trouble, real trouble. He shoves the window again, trying to ignore the pain in his arms. He wishes he were bigger, stronger. 'It won't open, Sam, it won't.'

'I don't think I can get up there, Riley, I'll fall off. I feel a bit dizzy from that smack on the head. You have to use all your might. I know it's scary and hard but try again. You can do it. I know you can.' Sam holds up his hands like he's actually pushing against the window, nodding his head like he knows that Riley can open the window if he just keeps trying.

Riley wants to sit down and cry, but he doesn't want to let Sam down. They can't stay locked up here. The police will never find them and then maybe they'll both just die down here. He'll never see his mum or Benji again. At this thought he gets angry and he gives the window an extra hard shove. It moves and opens, a small gap appears and the cold night air blows in. Riley shoves again and again, harder. His hands are getting sore.

'It won't move anymore. I can't fit through there,' says Riley, despair making him sink onto his haunches on the desk.

'Hell,' says Sam, 'now wait a minute. You can't fit through but Scotty can. Just wait.' He finds some paper and a pen in the mess on the desk and writes a note that he wraps around Scotty's collar as best he can. 'Hope it doesn't fall off.' Riley watches how Sam's hands shake, hoping that whoever finds the note will be able to read the old man's writing. His back is damp with sweat and he wants to cry but Sam's not crying so he has to be brave as well.

Sam hands the dog to Riley and then he reaches up and touches the little dog's head. 'Now, Scotty, you need to find Beverly, find her quickly, get Beverly, Scotty, get Beverly, quick, quick. Put him through there, careful now.'

Riley pushes Scotty through the gap in the window, careful not to hurt him. Once he's on the ground outside the window, the little dog looks at them, unsure what to do.

'He doesn't understand,' whispers Riley, on the verge of tears.

'Find the rabbit, Scotty,' says Sam, 'find the rabbit.'

The little dog's ears prick up and he looks around him and then chases after the imaginary rabbit.

Riley pulls the window closed but he can't close it completely. He climbs off the desk and together he and Sam move it back to where it was in silence.

'I don't think it's going to work,' says Riley. He can't hold back a few tears and he rubs his cheek on his shirt, not wanting Sam to see.

Sam sinks down onto the sofa and Riley can see he's not feeling good. He keeps rubbing his eyes. 'There's a hole in the fence that he sometimes creeps through if I don't watch him. I had some chicken wire there but it's come away and I was going to fix it tomorrow. I bought the supplies today even though Liza said shouldn't be doing it. If he finds the hole, he will go through and run into another garden. Maybe yours but, if not, someone else may find him and maybe read the note and then they will bring him back. I'm afraid that's the best we can hope for, lad. But I'm sure the police are looking everywhere. You mum won't rest til you're found. I know her.'

Sam speaks slowly as if he has to think really hard to find the words. Riley knows he should let him rest but he needs to talk to him. Sam's eyes start to close. Riley doesn't want him to be asleep. He needs to be awake.

'What if that woman is my mum? She keeps saying that. And she kind of… she kind of looks a bit like me. Our hair is the same colour and she has a chin like mine. I've been looking at her. Riley looks at the wall on the other end of the basement while he says this. It's painted but the paint is worn off in some places, red brick showing through. 'You said you believed her. Do you really believe she's my mum or were you just trying to trick her?'

Sam shakes his head. 'I don't… I don't think she's your mum… I was trying to get her to let us go or to get the police… but now… I don't know, lad. I might have a little rest.'

'No, Sam, stay awake, stay awake, please. We have to have another plan. If Scotty isn't found we need another plan.'

Sam shakes himself and rubs his eyes. 'All right then, let's strategise.'

Riley casts a hopeful glance at the window, sending thoughts of finding his mum to Scotty, and then he sits down on the sofa next to Sam who reaches out and takes his hand. The old man skin is thin and his hand warm and Riley curls his fingers into Sam's because he and Sam are going to strategise and they're going to get out of here. That's all he's going to think about right now. The things the woman has said can't be true. They just can't be.

CHAPTER THIRTY-SIX

Beverly

Both constables are on their phones verifying the whereabouts of Mr Benton. Beverly cannot sit still. She is in the kitchen, cleaning and making yet more tea. She glances at the bottle of wine on the counter, wishing that this was an ordinary Thursday night, that she could be sipping wine while she and Riley eat dinner. The daily drudgery of raising a child made her question her life sometimes, but she has never wished her son away. *He'll be home soon. He has to be. Where are you, Riley? Where could you be? Has someone taken you? Has the past reared its head? Has someone taken you?* The questions continue to circle her head. There are two people who might want him if they knew about him. They are the only other two people on earth related to him. *Did they know?*

The night her brother died returns to her. Every year on the anniversary of his death, she takes Riley to the cemetery where they visit the graves of his grandparents and his uncle. *His uncle.*

The night James died, the night he was killed, she had sat in the dark with her whisky, self-pity and despair, the overwhelming grief keeping her chained to the kitchen floor as she waited for her phone to have enough battery. She knew she should reach up and try to turn it on again, but her arms felt too heavy. She felt she would be on her kitchen floor forever. The energy to get up and try and find out where her nephew was somehow felt impossible to find.

She had seen Georgia running with something blue, something she had assumed was a onesie, but what if Georgia was actually running with the baby? She'd been across the road and quite far away when she caught sight of her.

As she lit another cigarette, a realisation slammed into her, making her slump even further down on the floor. She hadn't told the police about the baby. She had been hysterical and then in total shock. They would be looking for him right now if she had said something.

The police were searching for Georgia, but they had no idea about a baby, just that Beverly had seen her running from the building. She knew she needed to think properly, to think clearly about what to do. The first thing she needed to do was call the police and tell them the baby was missing, because he could be anywhere. Maybe he was with a neighbour and now Georgia had the baby. Did she stab James because he wouldn't tell her where the baby was, or because he told her and she got angry? Perhaps she had taken the baby and disappeared. Her mind spun with it all.

Beverly had told the police everything she knew about Georgia but when it came down to it, she didn't know very much at all, not even her surname. Still, they would find her. Someone would know more than she did. She reached up and grabbed her phone, knowing that it would be charged just enough for her to make a call, but when she tried to turn it on, the screen refused to light up and after trying twice more, Beverly threw the phone across the room, frustration and fear and anger all filling her body until there was no way to think straight, no way to know what to do, no way to cope except to give in to more tears.

Finally, her sobbing ceased and she took another sip of the whisky. She crawled across the kitchen and picked up her phone,

relieved to see it still intact, and then she plugged it in again before
sinking back onto the floor, grateful she was able to take another
sip of whisky. James would have texted her to tell her where his
son was and if he was still with a neighbour, she would have to
go back to that building, back to where her brother lost his life.
She would need to go back and get her nephew unless… Georgie
had him already. Unless she had him and she'd disappeared with
him forever. She shuddered at the thought, overwhelmed by it all.

She took another sip of the whisky, acid rising in her throat,
forcing her to swallow twice. She hadn't eaten for hours and her
head was feeling fuzzy but she didn't mind. Enough alcohol would
make it all go away and then she would sleep and then maybe she
could deal with finding her nephew.

'I can't,' she whispered to herself in her dark kitchen. 'I can't.'
She wasn't capable of dealing with anything.

She had a feeling she was never going to see her nephew again.
A great dark hole of aloneness opened up inside her. The collection
of sleeping pills she still had from when her parents died came to
mind – the white, blue and pink box hovered in the air in front of
her. James had doled them out one by one when she hadn't slept
for several nights in a row, but she hadn't used them for a good
year or so. They might still work. Enough of them might still work.

Beverly took a long drag of her cigarette and held the smoke
down in her lungs, feeling the burn, her eyes tearing up again.
She held the smoke there, holding it all inside her. The house was
silent and she was silent.

And in that silence, she heard a sound, a tiny mewling cry. She
shook her head, thinking she had imagined it. She brought the
cigarette to her lips again, enjoying the slight rush that holding her
breath with a lungful of smoke had given her. The cry was repeated.

It sounded like it was coming from inside the house. A light
moment of adrenaline washed over her, allowing her to find the
energy to get off the kitchen floor. Taking her cigarette, she walked

round, stopping every now and again to hold her breath and listen. She welcomed the distraction, knowing that the minute he stopped moving, she would see her brother again, his eyes open and glazed, his chest absolutely still. She felt too numb to cry anymore but she understood that in the coming hours, days, weeks and months, there would be nothing but tears. She knew he would never stop.

Walking past the spare room she noticed that the door was closed. It had been her father's study and then it had been a room for visiting friends, with a single bed and boxes of stuff that she was going to get rid of one day. For some reason she leaned her ear up against the door and waited; she heard the cry again, just softly, her heart hammering in her chest, her hands slightly shaky. She hoped it was a cat, because it could be a cat. The neighbours all had cats and she often found one of them wandering around her garden in the early mornings. She tried to remember if she had left the window open, knowing that it didn't have the protection of an insect screen. James was planning on fixing it soon, at least before summer began. The terrible, shocking recognition that James would not be there in summer made Beverly's knees tremble and sag, and she nearly, very nearly, resumed her position on the floor, but something made her keep standing.

Taking a deep breath, she opened the door and she was hit with the stench of him. Urine, faeces, vomit, all wrapped up together in one sickening smell.

'Oh God,' she uttered while her stomach churned. The baby was on the bed surrounded by pillows for protection.

Beverly held her breath, stepped gingerly into the room, walking slowly over to the baby as he raised one tiny fist up to the air. His soft, desperate cry came again. He was moving just a little, only a little, and she tried to think how many hours he had been there, alone, hungry and scared. Why didn't James tell her he left him here? Why would he have said nothing? How long had the baby been alone? Too many hours. Too many. 'Go home,' he kept telling her, 'go home.' He had thought she would go straight home from work. He had imagined she would immediately find the baby. She gasped, her phone… her battery was flat, he had asked and been angry about it when she arrived at the apartment. Why hadn't he called the store then? She experienced a moment of rage at her dead brother but then the baby wailed again, spurring her forward, energy surging through her.

'Think, Beverly, think,' she shouted, leading to more mewling from the baby. At least he was still alive, at least he was crying, if only a sad desperate wail.

She should call the ambulance and the police, but the most important thing was food. He needed food. She was so grateful that she was able to mix up the formula James had bought in the hope that one day he would have him long enough to feed him. She wasn't able to get the tin open as her hands shook and she took a knife, pushing it into the rim and cursing when it slipped sideways and scratched her skin, producing ruby-red little drops of blood. Relief whooshed through her body when the tin was finally open and then she had to read the instructions aloud so she would get it right, knowing the baby was starving, knowing that he needed her. She bit down on her lip, the pain making her focus after she spilled some of the powder. If he didn't suck, she would call the ambulance. She would call immediately. Her feet moved her quickly back to the room where he lay after she allowed the water in the kettle to heat up a little, hoping that since it had been boiled in the morning it was still fine to use. Her knowledge of what to do was limited but she moved the teat along his lips, imitating mothers she had seen on television, and his mouth clamped itself to the bottle. As he drank, his arms moved and she could see two tiny spots of colour in his cheeks.

'I'm so sorry, love, so sorry,' she whispered to him as he drank. She lifted him up afterwards, when he had quenched his thirst knowing that he had swallowed it too quickly and he would spit some of it back up. And he did, all over her hospital-provided scrubs, making her laugh, actually laugh, because she had not been quick enough.

She was sweating and still slightly sticky from the blood she had touched and now there was spit-up in her hair and down her back and he was drenched in a heavy nappy with a mess all up his back.

'What a pair we are,' she said to him. His eyes were closing so he must have held a reasonable amount of food down.

She took off his dirty clothes and laid him on the floor of the bathroom and ran a cool bath before taking off her own clothes and climbing in with him. She held him aloft as she dunked her head under the water.

She was gratified to see him kick his legs a little, to have the energy to enjoy the water. When they were both clean, she climbed out slowly, holding his wet, slippery small body carefully, and then she cocooned him in a large towel, wrapping him the way James had taught her to do, so that he would feel safe and secure, loved and protected.

She had a change of clothes and some nappies because James was always ready to babysit, and there was a portable cot that just needed to be assembled. In fact, as she looked around the spare room, the baby dozing in her arms, she realised that a lot of the baby's things were there, as though they had been brought over. Had James been planning to keep the baby with him for longer than a few days?

'Oh, James,' she whispered as she grabbed a warm onesie and a nappy, 'why didn't you tell me what you were planning? I would have helped.' Tears arrived again but she could see they upset the baby and so she stopped crying quickly, swallowing down her pain because she had to care for someone else.

When he was dressed and wrapped in a blanket, she laid him next to her and they slept together. All through the night as she fed

him and rocked him and changed him, she knew she was moving
towards a decision. In the morning, she was his and he was hers
and she would never let him go. She was not alone anymore.

That night, the night she found him, was the last time Beverly
had a cigarette. It amazed her that in the morning she had no
cravings for her drug of choice, no need for it. She had a baby and
there was no way that she would smoke around a baby.

It was easy enough to lie about him when the police came over
to interview her again, to ask the same questions over and over in
case there was a way she could be tripped up, even as they searched
for the real perpetrator, for Georgia.

'So you were at work the whole morning and you didn't take
break at all? And how long did you say it took you to drive from
work to the apartment? And you and your brother were close, no
arguments that morning?'

Beverly answered all the questions politely, seemingly patiently
even as she had to restrain herself from physically pushing them
out the door.

'I never took a break; you know that from Louisa. The drive
takes about ten minutes, then I parked and walked. Yes, we were
close, he was my brother. I loved him and we didn't argue. Why
are you talking to me when you should be looking for Georgia
– where is she?'

'She seems to have disappeared,' one of the constables told her.

Beverly sips some water as she thinks about the constables in
the other room right now, sitting on the same sofa another two
constables had sat on all those years ago. How can she be here
speaking to police about someone she loves being lost to her again?
Her stomach is a mess and what she would most like is for the
two constables here to just go away and leave her alone. Riley has
been missing for many hours now, but she doesn't know exactly

how many because she wasn't watching. She is a terrible mother, just awful, but she can't watch him every single minute. He was in his own backyard. He should have been safe, shouldn't he? They are still working on the theory that he may have run off because he was upset with her, but if that was the case, he would be home by now. It's nearly 10 p.m. and he will be starving. He was always starving anyway and she worried sometimes that his little body had intuited that food would not always be given to him when he was just shy of two months old, and had suffered alone and hungry while his father was murdered.

She is standing by the open kitchen door again, needing the fresh air, even though it's way too cold, and she's shivering in the light jumper she has on. But she cannot be in the same room as the constables because they both have a way of looking at her as though they know something. As if they are just waiting for her to admit what they are already aware of.

She should not have smoked a cigarette. She hasn't eaten because food is an impossible task and she is feeling really sick. Her mouth tastes thick and dark, and she has no idea how on earth she smoked for years, from the time she was fifteen.

In the interview with the police after James died, after she had answered all their questions again, a cry from the baby had alerted them to his presence and she knew that he couldn't be hidden from them. He had to be fed. She had brought him out and let them hold him while she prepared a bottle, the story she would tell them appearing as if by magic.

'There were baby things at the apartment,' the policewoman with blonde hair, cut short and tucked behind her ears, said.

'James was a good… good uncle,' Beverly had said, biting down on the word 'was', dropping her head so there was no way to see the lie there. 'Sometimes he and Georgia would babysit for me so I could get some rest. But only when they were kind of friendly with each other. It hasn't happened for a while. They've been fighting more and more. I don't think she liked doing it. That's why they were fighting. I mean, he wanted to break up with her, but I don't think... I don't know really. I just know that he thought she was behaving very strangely.' The lies slipped easily into the air, becoming the truth.

'You're very young to have a baby,' said the other constable whose slightly red nose and wrinkled eyes told of too much alcohol after her day was done.

'It was a one-night stand and James... well, he said he would help me raise him.' Her face flushed and she hoped they would read that as shame for her mistake, rather than fear over the lie.

'There's no record of you having a baby.' The constable's voice betrayed her scepticism and Beverly had to think fast. She didn't have the whole story yet and she hadn't realised they would have scrutinised her life that closely. But obviously they would have – her brother had been murdered.

'No... I had him at home.' That was true because he had been born in the house, in the bathroom with only her and James there because Georgia mistrusted hospitals who wanted to give children shots and tell parents how to feed them. The baby had no name, had not been registered and had yet to have his first vaccinations. Georgia begged James to wait on everything. 'I need to see who he is before I name him. It's better to wait on vaccinations, I've read that.' James argued but eventually accepted her decisions, needing her to stay calm, needing her to keep allowing him to see the baby. Beverly had not been able to believe that it was possible to have a child and have no one know. James had begged Georgia to go to a hospital for the birth but she refused. James and Beverly helped her deliver the baby at home and his safe arrival was all that mattered at the time.

There was even a small amount of blood that had stained the grouting on the bathroom floor, stubbornly refusing to come off.

She showed the constables, pretending pride at her achievement in doing it herself.

'You really should have registered the birth. And you didn't have a midwife?' Beverly could see the disbelief in the constable's eyes. She shook her head and rounded her shoulders, trying for sympathy.

'No… I wanted to… I was embarrassed and then… I left it too late. I wasn't sure what to do… Am I in trouble?'

Her mother used to say that she was a lovely little actress. She didn't know what her mother would have made of her then, but she had her reasons for her lies. Terrible people don't come from nowhere. The people Georgia came from were not good people. They would want the baby. They would snatch him from her and raise him the way they had raised their daughter. She would not let that happen.

'You have sixty days to register the birth. You should do that. You can get help from the government because you're a single mother. What's his name?'

She had smiled because it wasn't even a question. 'Riley, after my dad Ralph. Ralph felt like it was for an old man, but I like Riley.'

There was a lot of smiling and nodding.

And when the doctor's office called a few days later, she was able to tell the same story after she had explained away missing the appointment, 'No – there's no Georgia. Actually, James made it for me, for me and my son. I had him at home but he needs his vaccinations.'

A lie became the truth, but now… Now, all these years later, she has no idea what to do. Would telling the truth make any difference at all? *Has he run away? Has he been taken?* She thinks about the only other people in the world who would care that he exists, but they don't know about him, unless, unless they did know.

As Beverly watches over the dark garden, bats fly over, making their way to the park as they do every night searching for food. Their screeching sounds always alert her to the time and she knows she needs to get to bed so she can have some time to read and decompress from her day, but sleep is not even a possibility with her boy out there somewhere. *If he doesn't come home…* She refuses to finish the thought.

In the garden she sees movement across the lawn, but because it's so dark she can't see what it actually is. She steps back a little, almost inside the kitchen, ready to slam the door if it's something that is attracted to the light. She's found a possum in the kitchen before on a summer evening when she was letting in a breeze that had blown up.

Now a cold wind is gusting through the kitchen and there is some animal in the garden and she really needs to close the back door. She's been keeping it open – not just for the fresh air and so that she can smoke outside, but in the hope, the slim hope, that Riley will simply walk back in, a sheepish look on his face at his overreaction to not being allowed to play with the anonymous gift. *Who sent the gifts? Does the person who sent them have him? Mr Benton? But what reason could he have?* She has already made up her mind to get him one – one from her. After today she will buy Riley whatever he wants. She just needs him back here safe, with her.

The creature moves quickly and she steps back again, her hand on the door handle. Then it's right at the bottom of the concrete step and she gasps because it's Scotty.

She leans down and picks up the dog who leaps into her arms, his little body trembling. 'What are you doing here, boy, what's wrong? What's wrong? Why aren't you with Sam?'

'Who's that?' asks Constable Rivers, coming into the kitchen and automatically stepping forward to stroke the little dog's head.

'It's my neighbour's dog. He sometimes gets into my garden. They live at the back. There's a tree branch that's broken a section of the fence, but he's too small to climb over that – there must be a hole somewhere. Can I take him back to Sam? He's an old man and he must be worried about him.'

'Sure.' Constable Rivers smiles, her eyes crinkling as she continues to stroke Scotty's head and his little tail wags madly. I'll come with you.'

'Oh,' says Beverly, because she would love to just have five minutes on her own. The detective coming to speak to her has been delayed and she's promised not to leave the house. They believe she has something to do with Riley's disappearance. It's obvious they do. She has watched the two of them putting it together in the last few hours. Constable Riyad has had some whispered conversations with his wife, letting her know he wouldn't be home until very late, and Constable Rivers also appears to have spoken to someone about not coming home on time. Perhaps Beverly's youth or her jittery behaviour has alerted them to something, which they have assumed means she knows more about Riley's disappearance than she is saying. She does, and yet she doesn't.

'It will only take me a minute,' she says, 'just a minute.'

'That's okay, I don't mind the walk,' says the constable, her voice deliberately casual, and Beverly sighs. She really wanted a moment alone.

'Lisa,' calls Constable Riyad from the other room.

'Back in a sec,' she says to Beverly who nods as if she's going to wait, but instead walks quickly out of the kitchen door and down the back garden.

It's a bit awkward to clamber over the fallen branch with the dog in her arms but she manages and is grateful that there is a floodlight in Sam's back garden that comes on as she walks. The street lights don't provide much light and despite the full moon the garden seems like a collection of dark shadows. She decides to go around to the front door instead of knocking on the French doors that she knows lead to Sam's living room from the garden. She doesn't want to startle him.

She puts Scotty down and he trots alongside her, happy to be back in his own space. At the front door she rubs her arms, wishing she had stopped for a warmer jumper, but she'll only be a few minutes. She pushes the bell and waits.

'Where's Sam, Scotty?' she says to the little dog who looks up at her expectantly.

'Just coming,' she hears from inside the house, but it doesn't sound like Sam. She thought Liza was only coming in a couple of weeks.

'Riley's going to be so happy Thea and Amy are here,' Beverly says to Scotty and then she clenches her fist tightly. *Of course they're going to find him. Kids don't go missing. He's just run away. He'll be back and then… he's definitely grounded. Or he's getting presents or she'll just hug him forever.* She has been repeating these words to herself for the last few hours, convincing herself and the universe that by tomorrow this will all be over and that Riley will have caused a lot of fuss for nothing.

The door finally swings open and Beverly feels her breath catch in her throat as she recognises and yet doesn't recognise the woman standing before her. Shock ripples through her, forcing a gasp from her lips as she remembers the police returning a month after James was killed. She remembers the sombre look on their faces and the terrible news they told her. It had reaffirmed her decision to keep Riley, to make him hers. But now she cannot quite believe who she's looking at because there can be no doubt.

'You're—' she says and then her words disappear as her brain struggles to comprehend what she's seeing.

The police are looking into Mr Benton but Mr Benton is just a teacher who's a little nosy. Mr Benton doesn't have Riley. Riley is here, in this house.

She cannot find the words because her thoughts won't organise themselves.

'You'd better come in,' says the woman.

CHAPTER THIRTY-SEVEN

stand up and drain the last of the wine in my glass. A mother needs to have some time to relax but now it's time for me to get back to them, to make sure they've had the juice. I am going to struggle to get him upstairs because he's quite heavy and children seem heavier when they are deeply asleep. I remember him when he was a baby asleep in my arms, milk-drunk and content. He would grow heavier each moment I held him, but I never wanted to put him down.

The doorbell rings and I sigh. The police are obviously doing another round. I smile widely so that the right look is fixed in place and open the door.

And she's standing there. Beverly. The woman who stole my son. The woman who has kept him from me for eight, nearly nine years, and I wish her gone with a visceral force that makes me clench my fists. She shouldn't be here. I watch her connect the dots, make the connection, and I see understanding on her face.

'You're—' she begins.

'You'd better come in,' I say because I don't want her standing outside where the searching police will see her.

I don't show fear and I don't show her my dismay. I invite her in as I plan my next move. I remind myself that I am the one in control here. As I lead her to the kitchen, she follows me, too stunned to argue.

She is completely shocked to see me, but she recognises me, I can see that she does. She's putting two and two together, but I

don't think she's coming up with the correct answer. Scotty trot
along beside her, happy to be home again. How did they get him
out? What did they think the dog would achieve? Whatever it was
he has brought her to me. The knife is on the kitchen table and
grab it quickly, shoving it into my jeans at the back, ready for use

I wanted to leave, to just get him into a cab and leave, but no
I'm going to have to deal with her and Sam. If they were cleve
enough to get the dog out of there, I doubt they've drunk thei
juice. And now it's all going to be very complicated. Because I'n
going to need time to finish all this off, and it's three against one
I've always felt like that, like I have to fight the whole world fo
my happiness.

I smile and say, 'You'd better sit down.'

I see myself weeks from now, sitting with my parents, sippin
a glass of wine while Riley plays with his little black dog. There
no way they can be left alive now and it wouldn't be fair to leav
the dog without anyone to care for him. It wouldn't be fair at al

Her face is pale and grows paler as I take the knife out and shov
it to her. She stands with her back pressed against the fridge as w
assess each other in silence. I am bigger than her and I will easil
overpower her. I remember her as quite a chubby girl, but she i
small and thin now. She's actually quite pretty and I allow myse
the joy of imagining the mess the knife will make of her face.

'Sit down,' I command.

'I don't… don't—' she stutters.

'Sit down,' I tell her again and she leaves her safe space at th
fridge and sinks into one of the kitchen chairs.

'We have a lot to discuss,' I say, waving the knife in the ai
letting the light catch the steel. 'A lot to discuss.'

CHAPTER THIRTY-EIGHT

Beverly

As she slumps into a chair and stares at green eyes she recognises, Beverly's body shakes, her hands feel numb and she gulps in air. The moment she found her brother, more than eight years ago, after casually walking from the lift to his apartment, returns to her yet again, her slight hesitation when she saw that the door was open. *He knows I'm coming up. We'll go and get the baby together. I'll have to cancel my shifts at work so I can babysit.*

Georgia was gone and James was on the floor, blood seeping into a great pool on the grey carpet from the wound on his neck. Paralysed by shock, she had stood there staring down at him until she understood exactly what she was looking at.

'James, wait, no, wait, James!' she had screamed, crouching down next to him, her hand touching his neck. 'Just wait, hang on, hang on.' She leapt up and grabbed the landline, called 000, screamed into the phone, 'He's dying, he's dying.'

She had hauled the blanket off the couch, pressed it against his neck, moaned aloud as the blood soaked into the chocolate-brown fluff. She didn't understand where it all came from. How could there be so much blood?

When the paramedics arrived with the police, he was already gone, was already gone when she found him. He was bigger than Georgia, stronger than she was, but it doesn't take much to slice open a neck.

'Step back now,' the paramedics had shouted all at once.

Now, Beverly stares at a face she knows but does not know, a eyes she recognises but does not recognise.

'What?' is all she can think to say.

'That's exactly how I felt,' says the woman. 'All those years ag when I realised what had happened. It's exactly how I felt and it' how you deserve to feel.'

'Where's my son?' says Beverly, casting a quick glance at th kitchen door, wishing that she had Constable Rivers with her righ now, but sure the policewoman could only be moments behin her. The officer knows where she's going. If she doesn't return Constable Rivers will come looking for her. *Come looking for me please come looking for me.* This woman has her son. She know that without a doubt. 'Where's my son? Where's Riley?'

'Your son?' The woman's face twists and her lips curl, barin slightly crooked teeth. 'You know that's not true, don't you? You'r a liar who stole another woman's child and passed him off as you own. Where did you get to, Scotty? I thought you were downstairs The woman leans forward and pats the little dog. The pats ar more like hits, too hard, and Scotty immediately runs off. Beverl senses that she is not in the presence of someone sane, not at al

'I...' begins Beverly, but she has no idea what to say. 'The polic are looking for him. I told them I was coming here... I told ther I was bringing Scotty back. They'll be here in a moment.' She ha no idea if it is a good idea to tell her this or not, but perhaps she knows the police are coming, she will show her where Rile is, show her and let them go home. *Is he safe? Is my little boy okay Please God let him be okay.*

'Oh, I'm happy to explain it all to the police. You'll go to ja and I'll get custody of Riley.' The woman smiles, her voice fille with confidence, too much confidence, as though she is unawar that she has kidnapped a child.

'Where's Sam?' Beverly asks, remembering that he had told her he was going home and he would call her if Riley was there. A horrible thought crosses her mind. *Has she hurt Sam?*

'Sam is with Riley. No point pretending I don't have him. I mean, you recognise me, don't you, Beverly? I certainly recognise you, although you've aged a little. Being a mother is hard, but don't worry, I'm here to take him off your hands. He's coming with me now and I'll raise him the way he should have been raised. He'll have grandparents and a lovely home. You can leave and we'll forget that you stole him. I won't report you to the police.' She smiles, nodding a little, pleased at how nice she is being, and then she gives Beverly a quick wink, as though they are in this together. Fear makes its way around Beverly's body – she has no idea what this woman is capable of, how far she will go to get what she wants.

'That's… ridiculous,' says Beverly. Her voice is shaking along with her body. She can't quite catch her breath and she keeps glancing at the kitchen door, expecting to hear the constable coming up the front pathway to Sam's house.

'No,' says the woman, her smile disappearing, her voice cold. Ridiculous is assuming that you would get away with keeping a child who didn't belong to you. I didn't believe it at first. I found you on Facebook and I wasn't even looking, but there you were, looking pleased as punch with yourself even though you knew you were a hideous criminal. I googled you and found the library where you work; it's so close to the house you and James lived in eight years ago – I knew you hadn't moved. You really should have moved.'

Beverly takes refuge in silence, not knowing what to say or how to get herself out of here with her son. This cannot be happening and yet here she is and this woman has Riley.

'I want to see him,' Beverly says, careful not to call him her son, knowing that will anger the woman holding the knife. If she

can just see Riley then she can plan what to do. The police wi
be here soon. They absolutely have to be. If she can be sure Rile
is safe, she can wait until they ring the doorbell and then she wi
scream her lungs out. But first she needs to see Riley.

'I'll take you to him. Stand up and follow me.'

Beverly is the fly in the spider's web, trapped and unable t
free herself. She stands up.

'Good,' says the woman as though Beverly has done somethin
she wanted her to do. 'Now follow me, come on.' The knife is i
her hand and she uses it to gesture. 'Actually, you go in front. It
the basement. That's where they are. Do you know how to get t
the basement? If not, I'll show you.'

The woman comes to stand behind Beverly who cannot seer
to make her feet move. Her heart is racing and her mind is ju
a confusion of jumbled thoughts. The woman shoves her a littl
and Beverly begins to walk towards the back of the house wher
she knows the basement is.

'Come on, move now,' she says as though speaking to a chilc
'You want to see him, don't you? You want to see your *son*.'

Beverly can hear the emphasis on the word 'son'. She wants t
sink to the floor and moan in terror, but she keeps moving wit
little shoves from the woman.

She takes small, slow steps. *Where are the police? Why aren't th*
here yet? Constable Rivers, where are you, where are you? Beverl
stops when she hears the woman pick up something from a tab
in the living room. She turns to see what it is.

The movement of hands is a blur and the mallet comes dow
so quickly she has no idea where it even came from. She stagge
and then feels her knees crumple. A second later, she is on th
ground and there is nothing else.

CHAPTER THIRTY-NINE

This is a very handy mallet. I contemplate hitting her a few more times, just to be done with it. But I want her to wake up and tell Riley the truth. I need to get her away from here, away from the living room, with its easy view to the front door, and down into the basement. When the police come, I can say she never arrived here. I practise a look of confusion. 'But Sam is away,' I will say. 'Scotty has gone with him. It couldn't have been Scotty.'

I sink down into a chair near the door to the basement. It's the chair where Sam leaves Scotty's lead. I am exhausted from all this now. This is getting harder and harder. *How did Scotty get out? Have they found a way out?* I stand up and grab the lead, flip Beverly over and tie up her hands as tightly as I can, and then I drag her closer to the basement door. It's only a few feet away and she's light enough. When she wakes up, I will force her to tell the truth and then Riley and I can leave. I don't really like the name Riley. I think he's more of a Ben. It was the name I suggested when he was first born but I wasn't listened to.

One more hit should end Sam's life and a couple more will sort out Beverly, but if not I have the knife. I know one slice across her neck will stop everything very quickly. I smile as I contemplate putting the knife in Sam's hand and imagine what the police will make of that.

I feel my brain firing with all sorts of solutions now. It's better when I feel this way, as though a smarter part of me has taken over. I remember that part of me taking over the last time I saw my parents on that cold winter's night. I remember realising tha all I needed to do was bring them the son I had just found ou about, the boy I believed was gone. I stood there for hours. It wa very cold and I don't recall what time I left, only that I felt bette about things afterwards.

I unlock the basement door and there at the bottom of th stairs are Sam and Riley, looking as though butter wouldn't mel in their mouths as they watch television on the sofa. But I knov that somehow they got Scotty out of here. I glance at the lon thin window and it's obvious that it's been opened. Clever them A slight chill blows through the room at least, making thing smell better.

'Look who came to visit,' I say and they both stare at me as pull Beverly's body to the top of the stairs.

'Mum,' whispers Riley, his eyes wide and his face pale. His bod starts rising from the sofa, his hands curling into fists.

'Not Mum,' I say, grunting slightly with the effort of movin her. 'She is not your mum,' I say as I position her at the top c the stairs. 'I'm your mother.' I push her and her body slump forward down two or three stairs. Scotty scampers past me an bolts down the stairs.

I don't stay to watch what happens. I shut the door, lockin them all in. I will wait until the police have come and gone an then I will deal with all three of them.

At that exact moment, the bell rings. I square my shoulde and paste on yet another smile.

The policewoman at the door is different to the other two.

'I'm looking for Beverly Cochran,' she says. 'She found a dog a little black dog, and she said he lived here. She was coming t return him to the owner. Are you the owner? She said it was an ol man.' The words come out in a rush and I can see she's panting little. She must have run over when she realised that Beverly wa here. Too bad she didn't run fast enough.

Keeping my ears tuned for any shouting coming from the basement, I tell the story of being the dog-sitter, instead of saying that Sam has taken Scotty to Melbourne with him. 'I am actually worried about Scotty so I'm grateful that she's found him, but she hasn't come here. Are you sure she said she was coming to return him?' The story pops into my brain, the perfect story. I frown a little so she knows I'm really worried about the dog.

'She definitely said she was coming here,' says the policewoman. 'Are you sure she's not here?'

There is always a moment when you are lying when you can make a mistake, a small slip that alerts the other person. I don't want to make that mistake so I'm careful.

I repeat, 'She definitely didn't come here.' Then I throw the focus on to her. 'Are you feeling okay? You look a bit pale.' She doesn't but the mind is a powerful thing and as I watch her, the colour in her cheeks fades somewhat. 'Would you like a glass of water or something?' I step back as if to allow her into the house, indicating that I have nothing to hide, that I am merely the dog-sitter, merely the dog-sitter worried about where the dog is. I can see her processing the idea that I wouldn't invite her in if I had something to hide.

'No, I'm fine, thanks,' she says, unsure what to do now that I've proved myself truthful.

'I might go out and take a look around for Scotty. He's sure to wander home, but it is getting very cold and late. If you're looking for Beverly, could you keep a look out for him as well? Sam is so fond of him; I would hate to lose him because Sam loves him so much. I would never be trusted with anyone's dog ever again.' I shake my head and rub my arms as the cold wind blows into the house. 'You know what it's like when you're taking care of someone else's dog or child.'

'I do,' she says. 'Thanks, I'll keep looking.' She takes her phone out of her pocket and pushes it to her ear as she walks away. She's concerned about Beverly now and she's questioning herself. Sh should not have let Beverly out of her sight.

It's so easy to throw people's thoughts into disarray. I onl learned how to do that later in life but I learned it well. In genera human beings have a tendency to question their own thought ideas and opinions. Few people always believe they are absolute right about everything and most of the time, just a few well-chose words can change everything.

And when you find those words, it becomes possible to imagin that all you've ever wanted in life can be yours. I found those word once, I nearly had everything I wanted before Beverly stole it awa That won't happen again.

CHAPTER FORTY
Riley

'Help me, Sam, I can't do it,' says Riley as he tries to lift his mum by her shoulders so he can get her down the stairs.

'All right, son, here I come, I'm coming,' says Sam but as he stands up his body moves like he's trying to dance and then he sits down again. 'Give me a moment, I'm just so dizzy, just a moment.'

Riley feels a scream bubbling up inside his throat. He is so scared and angry and worried about his mum and Sam, but he has to get her off the stairs. She is lying in a funny heap like a broken doll and her face is white and she looks weird. He grunts as he turns his mum around a little so her head is facing down the stairs and then he takes a deep breath and lifts her up, pulling her body down to the basement, hating the thump, thump, thump sound it makes.

When he gets to the bottom, he sits down, sweating with sore arms. Scotty comes over to his mum and sits down by her head and then he whines a bit like he's telling Riley to keep going.

'I'm so sorry, Riley… so sorry,' says Sam, and to Riley it sounds like he's having trouble taking a big breath.

He stands up and pushes his shoulders back so he feels bigger. 'It's okay, Sam, just stay there. I can do this.' He gets his hands and arms under his mum's arms and drags her along the carpet until he's lying next to the sofa and then he slumps down next to her. 'Wake up, Mum,' he whispers in her ear, but she doesn't move.

He puts his ear right by her mouth and feels her warm breath on his cheek. She smells like orange juice and tomato sauce. On his green shirt he can see some red and he knows for sure now that they were having spaghetti for dinner.

'What are we going to do now, Sam?' Riley says quietly because he's so tired and so sad. Scotty got his mum but the mad woman hurt her as well. *How many more people is she going to hurt?*

'I don't know, lad,' says Sam, shaking his head, 'I just don't know.'

Riley lies over his mum, wrapping his arms tightly around her. 'Wake up, Mum, please,' he says, squeezing her, and he lets himself cry even though he's trying to be brave and strong. His tears fall on her shirt and he holds on tighter, waiting – just waiting for her to put her arms around him and say, 'It's okay, sweet boy, it's okay,' like she usually does.

'All right, lad,' he hears Sam say. 'Come on now, come over here, it's all right. We'll figure it out, I promise, come sit by me. Have something to eat. Your mum will wake up soon and then we can figure out what to do.'

Riley does what Sam says but it doesn't feel like they're going to figure anything out. The mad woman will be back soon and it will be too late. He can feel it will be too late to figure anything out at all.

CHAPTER FORTY-ONE

Beverly

When Beverly surfaces, she is in Sam's basement with no clue as to how she got there. She moves slightly, feeling like she is bruised all over with no idea why that would be the case.

There is a sofa, upholstered in some dreadful seventies orange fabric, and Riley is sitting on it, staring at a television set as he mindlessly eats from a family-sized bag of chips.

'Riley,' she whispers and he stops eating, his gaze darting towards the door at the top of the steps. He slides off the sofa and comes to crouch next to her. 'Just pretend you're sleeping, Mum. She won't hurt you if you're sleeping. Me and Sam have a plan.' His stance has not been mindless at all. Instead, he has been waiting for her to wake up.

'I found Scotty,' she says. 'That's why I came.' A thumping ache makes her teeth hurt as she speaks.

'Yeah, but you didn't read the note on his collar. We pinned a note to his collar,' Riley says, his mouth dropping at the sides. He is disappointed in her.

'No, no I didn't, I'm… There wasn't a note. I'm so sorry. Oh, baby, are you all right?' She struggles to sit up but he pushes her down onto the floor.

'Shh, Mum, pretend to be sleeping. It's okay. We pushed Scotty through the window but if Sam breaks the glass, I can get through. He'll break the glass and I'll run and call for help.'

Sam looms into view above her and she gasps at the shocking black bruise that has spread across one whole side of his face.

'Looks worse than it feels,' he smiles, but he winces and she can see that he's keeping up a front for Riley.

The bruise is hideous and even as she watches it, it seems to grow. She lifts her head, but a pounding pain forces her to drop it back to the carpet. She hit her as well. That's how she got her in here. Beverly's whole head is an intense ache. She must have hit her. She wants to close her eyes but they have to get out of here. Only someone crazy would do this. But exactly how crazy is she?

'I'm so sorry, Sam. Oh God, what a mess. What are we going to do?' She bites down on her lip, not wanting Riley to see her cry.

'We'll figure it out, love, don't you worry,' says Sam. He leans down and rests his hand across her forehead and the simple, kind gesture forces tears down her cheeks.

'She's says she's my mum,' says Riley. 'Why would she say that?' He clasps his hands together, threading his fingers in between each other, something he does when he is frustrated and worried.

'She's… it's complicated, Riley, but there is something very wrong with her, obviously.'

An outright lie would be unacceptable. She can see that. The truth is coming out because it's been waiting to come out for eight years. All her secrets are about to be revealed and there's no way to stop that now. And now she knows exactly how much was concealed from her, concealed from James as well. Pieces of the puzzle are clicking into place, memories becoming clear as her understanding unfolds. If they had known, if they had suspected… she doesn't know what she would have done and there's no time to ruminate on that now.

First, Beverly needs to get them all out of here and to safety. She moves her head, looking around the room, and then she focuses on the window that she thinks Riley is talking about. It looks too small for her little boy to squeeze through even with

he glass broken, and there is no way to break the glass without
ummoning the woman upstairs with the noise. She can't let Riley
rawl through there. He will surely cut himself on shards of glass
nd she cannot allow him to get hurt. She has already let him
own far too much.

'The police will come looking for me soon, they have to. I told
hem I was taking Scotty back to Sam's house but I didn't…' She
tops speaking. She told Constable Rivers that Scotty belonged
o her neighbour behind her: to Sam. *Surely they won't be long?*

She struggles up onto her elbows, unsure if she should stand
p or not. In addition to the headache, she feels dizzy. She must
ave been hit really hard.

'Let's break the glass now,' says Riley. 'I'll run and get help.'

'I'm a bit worried about you getting hurt, Riley,' says Sam. 'And
still need to find something to break it with.' Beverly can see he's
ot into the idea. Riley must be pushing for it.

'We need her hammer,' says Riley. He stands up. 'Or I can just
mash it with my hand.'

'No, no, Riley, don't—' begins Beverly and there is the sound
f a lock being opened. Riley darts back to the sofa, his gaze fixes
n the television. Sam sits down on the sofa and Beverly drops
ack to the floor and closes her eyes. She has no idea what to do
ow but until she does, she'll keep her eyes closed.

CHAPTER FORTY-TWO

I open the door and look at where she is lying near the sofa. hope it was difficult for them to get her down the stairs. I hop she bounced off each stair and now her skin is bruised and painfu and ugly. I'm not a bad person but she did a very bad thing an she needs to be punished for it. The police will probably not se it that way. I have locked Riley up with Sam and I have hit bot him and Beverly. Police have their own way of seeing things.

Her eyes are closed but I know she's awake. I heard them talkin

I walk slowly down the stairs, the mallet in my hand and th knife in my jeans. I am a warrior, armed to the teeth and read to defend what I love. I love my son and I have to get him awa from here so I can tell him the truth about his birth and his fathe and everything that happened.

I don't think about James much. I used to find him quite goo looking with his big brown eyes and messy dark-blond hair. Bu his face has faded because he has very little relevance to me nov He helped make Riley and that's pretty much it.

My heart is racing and I feel slightly sick. I have to hit her firs Sam and Riley will be easy to fight off but she might be hard worl It's best if she's no longer in the picture.

'Listen, my dear,' begins Sam, 'I think this has all gone f. enough now. It's time to let us all out of here. You won't get awa with this, you understand. The police will come looking and m daughter calls every night and if I don't answer the phone then sh sends the police out. She calls at nine on the dot and…' He stop

peaking as he glances at his watch. He shakes his head in disbelief.
t's way past 10.30 p.m. now. Perhaps she called or tried to call
ut his mobile phone is off and the home phone is disconnected.
This is not, as the saying goes, my first rodeo.

'The police have already been, Sam. I told them I was dog-
itting, so you see, they won't be back. They just won't. And Liza
s still in Melbourne. No one is coming to help any of you.'

From the floor, I hear a soft sigh of despair, of defeat. She
hought the police were coming. Sam drops his head as he also
eels the sting of defeat. But Riley, defiant Riley, locks eyes with
ne and I can see that right now he hates me with everything he
nas. That's fine. I have time to knock that out of him, years and
years of just the two of us, and in the end, he will love me as he
hould. Despite everything my parents did to me, I still love them,
till yearn for their approval. That's why I need a son. That's what
ne's for.

'I know you're awake, you know,' she hears. Beverly opens her eyes. In one movement she rolls on her side and stands up, her movement awkward because of her tied hands, her muscles aching and her head thumping. She feels a pull of tension along her neck and shoulders.

'You need to let us go,' she says firmly, hoping that she has control of her voice, that her fear is not obvious. It's three against one but Sam is an old man and he's hurt. Riley is strong but the woman is big and tall. And Beverly's hands are tied.

'No… no,' says the woman. 'I don't need to do anything like that.'

She meets Beverly's gaze with her own green-eyed stare and a chill ripples up Beverly's spine. They are in grave danger here, but she's not about to let anything happen to her son. Despite her tied hands and the fact that the woman is holding a mallet and has a knife in her pants, Beverly cannot help a surge of anger.

'What do you think you're going to do here? What exactly are you hoping to achieve? You can't keep us locked up in here. The police know where I am, you know. They'll be here any minute. This is insane. Even if they have already been they will come back. They are looking for Riley and now they're looking for me.'

The words trip off Beverly's tongue even as she watches the woman's face redden with her own fury. She knows she shoul top but she can't seem to stop. She thinks about everything she knew about Georgia and her parents and realises that there was much more that was hidden from her and James. The woman in front of her means to do more harm than just taking Riley and claiming him as her son. Beverly watches the way her hands tighten on the mallet and knows that she intends to use it again. She and Sam are not meant to live to see another day. Her brother's face, her brother's voice, are in her mind. *Don't let her have my son, Bev, don't let her take him.* She wriggles her hands, trying to loosen whatever they are tied with, cursing herself for not instructing her son to untie her earlier on.

'What's insane is stealing someone else's child,' says the woman as she calms herself with a deep breath.

Beverly feels her jaw tense. 'I'm telling you to let us go, let us go now! The police are coming.'

Her voice rises because she needs someone, anyone, to hear them. She contemplates simply shouting and screaming for help, hoping that the police are just outside. She pictures Constable Rivers walking up Sam's front path, knocking on the door to come again and then hearing her scream.

'Oh, Beverly, Beverly,' laughs the woman, 'they've come and gone. You don't believe me but they have. A policewoman came to find you and I told her…' she starts to giggle, delighted with her cleverness, 'I told her to keep a lookout for Scotty.'

Scotty barks in recognition of his name.

'Shut it,' hisses the woman, all traces of mirth disappearing. She doesn't want any noise.

Beverly wonders if anyone will hear her scream from the basement. It's possible, if she screams loud enough, it's possible. She pictures police roaming the neighbourhood, looking for Riley and now for her. They will know she's close. Surely Constable Rivers will keep looking for her, will suspect something strange is going on. She needs to make as much noise as possible.

She takes a breath.

'If you scream, I will hurt him,' says the woman, grabbing Riley who immediately tries to wriggle away until she drops the mallet on the floor and pulls the knife from her jeans. She holds the sharp blade to the front of his throat and Riley freezes, his eyes wide with incomprehension. There is a knife at his throat. An actual knife, pointed and deadly in the basement light.

This cannot be happening. Her desire to scream disappears. 'I won't scream, just… please,' begs Beverly, 'please don't hurt him. You can do anything you want to me, just don't hurt him.' Her knees sag, fear making her sweat. 'Don't hurt him, don't hurt him,' she begs. She sends up a prayer to whoever is listening, a message to her brother to save his son. *Help us, James. She's going to steal him away and if she's willing to hurt him, she has no love for him at all. Please help us get out of this alive.*

'This is madness,' says Sam. 'He's just a little boy, put that down now.' Beverly can hear that he's trying to sound strong but his voice is light and weak and she feels his frailty in the air. Sam needs a hospital.

The police will be here soon, they have to be. They will return to this house where she said she would be. They are looking for her son and they will be looking for her now as well. She needs to keep this woman talking until they get here, that's all she needs to do.

Beverly moves her hands back and forth, back and forth, the skin chafing, her muscles aching. Slowly, carefully, so the woman can't see what she's doing. Whatever is holding her hands together loosens slightly.

'What's your name?' she asks and the woman smiles. She drops the knife away from Riley's throat, but still holds onto him.

'Didn't Georgia tell you about me?'

'No,' says Beverly, 'no, she didn't.'

CHAPTER FORTY-FOUR

Riley

Riley feels the woman's grip loosen. How can his mum not know who the mad woman is if she said that she was his mum? He looks at Sam who gives his head a little shake and Riley knows that Sam is telling him to keep still, to not do anything, but the need to move is a jumpy feeling inside Riley, like he's standing on a spring. If he stomps on the woman's toes and runs for the basement door, would he get away quickly enough? If he stomps on her toes and picks up the mallet at his feet, could he hit her?

When she threw his mum into the basement he got really, really scared that they would all die in here. The woman could just lock them up forever and leave them all to die. She says she's his mother and a mother is not supposed to hurt her child, but she hurt Sam and she hurt his mum so who knows what she would do.

'Don't lose it now, son,' Sam told him when he came to sit next to him on the sofa, after he dragged his mum down the stairs. Riley had swallowed his despair and he and Sam began planning what to do next when his mum opened her eyes. He wishes he had untied her straight away but maybe then that would have made the woman mad. Madder.

'Didn't Georgia tell you about me?' the woman asked his mum. He doesn't know who Georgia is. He's never heard that name before.

'My name is Heather,' I say.

'Heather,' she repeats.

'Yes, Heather, the older sister.'

'She never mentioned you,' says Beverly and I notice a slight movement of her shoulders. She is trying to undo her hands. I lift the knife again, nearer to Riley's throat, so she knows who's in charge, and before I even have to say anything, all movement stops. That's good. We are communicating without speaking now. She understands what I'm capable of.

'She never told us she had a sister,' says Beverly, her voice barely above a whisper.

'I know,' I say. 'I told her not to tell you.'

I don't say that Georgia told me, just before I left home, that she was going to tell everyone she was an only child. The pain of her words stayed with me for a long time. Not only did she not love me, but she simply wanted to erase me from her life. Later I realised that it was more than that. Georgia liked to be the centre of attention, her whole life revolved around her and even her painful childhood only had room for one person who suffered, one person who lived the experience, just her. But I don't tell that to Beverly. She has no right to know all my secrets.

'I didn't want you to know about me, you or James. I was a secret that she and I kept,' I say proudly.

I watch the pieces click into place. She didn't even know she was hiding Riley from me. She didn't know about the plan Georgia and I had, and then the plan that I had all alone… All alone and just for me.

CHAPTER FORTY-SIX

Beverly

Georgia never said she had a sister. She never said she didn't either. Having a brother named James was one of the first things Beverly told people about herself. He was integral to who she was and how she was raised. The moment she saw this woman, Heather, she knew she was related to Georgia. She is a taller, less pretty version of Georgia, but no less dangerous. The same green eyes and the same damage that made Georgia who she was, are also part of Heather.

'Why didn't you want me and James to know about you?' Beverly asks, her hands moving slightly, so slightly that Heather will not be tempted to raise the knife again. She wonders if she can get through to her, if she can keep talking until she makes a connection.

'Well, Georgia was never going to be capable of raising a child—'

'She had James to help, she had me,' says Beverly, wondering what Georgia's fitness as a parent had to do with anything.

'Stop moving and stop interrupting,' says Heather, the knife going back to Riley's throat.

'You keep saying you're his mother, but you're not and if you were, you wouldn't be trying to hurt him, you wouldn't be holding him the way you are. A mother doesn't do that.' She speaks softly knowing her words will anger the woman, but still hoping to get through to her.

'How would you know what a mother would and would not do, Beverly? You're not his mother.'

Beverly drops her head. 'You're lying,' she says.

'Mum?' asks Riley, shock and sadness in the single word. 'Mum, why does she keep saying that?'

'She's… lying, Riley,' says Beverly, but there is no force behind the words and she can see that her son is starting to question this fact. This one very important fact about who he is and his place in the world. Her heart breaks for him and she wishes she could just reveal it all, but right now she needs to get him out of here, to get them all out of here.

CHAPTER FORTY-SEVEN

Heather

I want to smack the lie right out of her mouth, force her to spit the truth out. But she won't confess until she has no choice. I need to convince her that she has no choice. But that is something I've become really good at doing.

I see my sister's pretty face, her lovely smile. I hated my sister. I hated my parents for who they were and what they did to us, and I hated my sister for not being someone I could count on, for being someone who perpetuated what they did to us by essentially becoming like them. I hated her for being so pretty and so clever, for everything really.

On the day I left home or, more accurately, on the day I was told to leave home, was told that my parents were done with taking care of my needs, I was packing my suitcase when she came into my room and sat on my bed. I was glad to be going but absolutely terrified about how I was going to live. I had some money from a part-time job and my parents had given me an envelope with a few hundred dollars, no doubt hoping that I would stay away forever.

Georgia was dressed in jeans and a white shirt, her long brown hair tumbling casually over her shoulders, her perfect lips light pink with lip gloss. I couldn't help comparing us. I was wearing a boiler suit because it was comfortable and my brown hair was

ulled back into a ponytail because it never did anything except
ang limply. I wasn't wearing any make-up because even though
was eighteen, I still suffered from terrible acne.

'Least I won't have to look at that face over dinner anymore,'
ny father said to me at breakfast that morning, leading to sniggers
rom Georgia.

I was ready to leave them all but when she came into my room
nd sat down on my bed, I had a moment of hope that she would
t least express a little bit of regret that I was going. I even had
isions of a nice goodbye card and maybe even a plan to meet up
nce in a while.

Slumped on my bed, she watched me for a few minutes and
nen she smiled her generous smile, which lifted her face from
retty into beautiful, and said, 'You've been a bit of a crap big
ster. No one is going to miss your miserable face. I'm going to
retend you never existed at all.' And then she got off the bed and
ounced out of the room. 'Maybe if your face clears up, you'll get
 shag,' she said from the doorway and then she giggled at her
ttempt at humour.

Georgia excelled at cruelty, as did my parents. I was used to
ruelty in my house. But it was the timing that broke my already
racked heart. I had wanted a few words of kindness, I hoped for
 gesture of some sort, but all she wanted was to make sure that I
nderstood I wasn't loved or wanted. All my life I have clung to
ne hope that someone, somewhere, loved me. I was wrong until
.iley was born.

I never went to university but I've read a lot of books. I could
ever afford therapy but I liked the psychology section of the
brary. I know that my sister's cruelty was simply a paying it
orward of my parents' cruelty.

It would have taken a very special person to transcend my
arents' disappointment in our existences. My sister had the
dvantage of looks and intelligence, but she could only use what

she had for cruelty. And she was never going to be the son the
longed for.

I didn't hear from her until about nine years ago. I kept tabs o
her through Facebook. I set up a fake account, gave myself a gener
name and then friended all her friends until eventually she mu
have thought she knew me. I never used a picture of myself, onl
sunrises and sunsets, and I threw in a lot of inspirational quote
about believing in yourself and rising above your pain. No on
worries about a person like that on Facebook. They're harmless

I drifted from job to job and had a couple of not very nic
boyfriends. I wanted, more than anything, to have a family.
wanted to have a husband and children. When I got to thirty,
thought that a husband would probably not be an option. I wa
not made for the modern dating scene. I fell in love too quickl
or rather I fell in love with the idea of having a husband and
family too quickly. Any man would have done, but in relationshi
I always pushed for things to move forward and scared men off.
was desperate. I needed to rewrite my history by being the moth
I never had. I couldn't find anyone willing to rewrite it with m

More than anything, I wanted a child. I wanted to mother
child in the way that my parents didn't want a child.

I started investigating sperm donation. I went for all the tes
and for the first time in my life, I was positive about the future.
had a job as an office manager then. It was one of the first decer
jobs I had and I was good at it. I'm a planner, an organiser, an
I did well. My co-workers kept their distance. I once overhear
one of them, a man of course, speaking about me in that horrib
dismissive way that men speak about women. I had asked him o
and when he told me he had a girlfriend, I told him I only wante
sex. I only wanted some biological contribution by then. He refuse
and I persisted until I heard him refer to me as 'Hideous Heathe
I stopped trying to find a man then and I started planning a ne
way to make myself a family. I knew sperm donation was the on

way forward and even though it would drain my savings, I had no choice but to try. The longing for a child was an ache inside me by then that coloured everything in my life. I scrolled through Facebook, looking at other people's children the way some men look at other woman. I became obsessed, even joining a few online mothers' groups with some lovely generic photos of a baby I knew would have one day.

Some days remain in your mind because they are wonderful, filled with the sweetness of good food and the laughter of friends, unexpected in their simple joy. Other days are coloured black and unforgettable because of the way they changed your life, the way they changed you from a human being living with hope to one utterly devoid of hope.

The day I went to see the gynaecologist to hear the results of my tests was a spring morning that pulsed with life; flowers opened their buds in the warmth and bare winter trees cloaked themselves in green. I entered the doctor's office, filled with optimism and hope, and I could see that the following spring I would be holding a newborn. I was going to achieve my dream of becoming a mother. I smiled at the receptionist as I sat down and picked up a woman's magazine, turning immediately to an advice page for new mothers. I would need all the help I could get but I knew I was going to be a wonderful mother.

'I'm afraid children won't be possible, Heather,' the soft-voiced gynaecologist told me as I sat opposite her in her lavender-scented office, her blue eyes filled with sympathy.

'But I'm only thirty-four,' I protested, as if she just needed to be told this fact and it would mean that she was wrong.

'I understand,' she said, touching her glasses to straighten them on her face. She went on to explain everything that was wrong with me – too many things to think about. What I came away with was the knowledge that I could have a child if I got a donor egg and donor sperm and maybe even a donor uterus. But all of that needed money, thousands and thousands of dollars. Thousands. My office manager job wouldn't cover the expenses. Even with Medicare and a health fund I couldn't afford it.

'Adoption is a wonderful way to give a child a home,' the doctor told me. But I didn't want to adopt. I was a single woman, earning a nice but not very big salary. No one was going to let me adopt a child and I didn't want to be a foster parent. I had no desire to try and undo the damage someone else's parents had caused. I had enough trouble managing my own damage.

I emerged from her office a shattered human being. The spring warmth was too hot, the sweet smell of flowers sickly. I wanted to die, to lie down in the street next to the potted plants outside her office building and die. All hope was gone. I dragged myself back to the bus stop and when a mother with a young child stood near me, my hands itched to grab the little girl and run. I saw how quickly it would happen, how easily I could reach for her and pull her away. But then the bus arrived and the mother leaned down and lifted the child onto her hip. 'Here we go, love,' she said as she climbed on the bus. I sank down onto the bench, waved the bus away and waited for the next one. I would never have a child. Never.

In the black weeks that followed, my boss, Lewis, tried to be sympathetic, but eventually I simply stopped returning his calls. I couldn't explain what was happening and I didn't have the energy to get myself to a doctor for a mental health plan and everything else I would need.

At thirty-four years old, I had lost my job, my prospect of becoming a mother and my will to go on with my life. I shut myself into my apartment, used my unemployment to make rent and lived on cheap food, waiting for death. That's all I could think of: the relief of not being here anymore, but at the same time I was too cowardly to take the final step.

And then, one night, a knock at the door that I assumed was my cheap takeaway pizza turned out to be my sister.

Her beautiful hair was cut short and even though she was only just thirty-three, there were creases around her mouth and nose. Life had worn her down and even through the darkness of my own despair I experienced a moment of smug joy that she too was unhappy.

'Aren't you going to invite me in?' she asked and she smiled; I saw the smile light up her pretty eyes so I stepped back and let her in.

That night will stay with me forever because of what she told me, of what we planned. It was the gift of returned hope. And I knew I needed to get her on my side, convince her of my desire to help, make sure she believed whatever I said.

And now I need to convince Beverly to tell the truth, the whole truth. I look at the three of them, knowing that there are only two people standing in the way of me and the life I have always dreamed of. There used to be four. Georgia took care of James, something I only learned a year ago when I started planning this.

And then Georgia... Well, now we're down to two. Such a small little number, just two. I don't want to hurt them but I have to. I cannot have my child taken from me again.

The police may search for him if they find them dead, but I will be long gone by then and no one will ever think to look for me. Few people knew I existed.

I need to get this done now.

I let Riley go and he steps away from me, his face pale. He touches his neck gingerly as though checking I haven't actually cut him with the knife.

'Now,' I say and I look around me. Sam's basement is full of treasures. He seems to have collected endless extension cords although I have no idea why he would need so many. I'm glad then I spot them. They're useful for tying people up. 'No one move,' I threaten as I move across the basement and grab a cord.

'Stand still, Sam.' I am enjoying the silence and the discomfor that hangs in the air. They have no idea what to do now as th clock moves towards eleven. Soon it will be a new day and I wi have a new life.

I try not to hurt Sam when I bind his wrists and I am kin enough to tie his hands in front of him, knowing that having h arms tied behind his back would be painful for an old man. H submits easily but it's awkward work with the knife in my han as well.

'Please explain, Heather, please tell me why you're doing this says Beverly.

She wants to keep me talking but I need to get on with thi She thinks I can't see the subtle movement of her hands workin on her untying, but I can. If they all rushed me at once, the could probably take me down, but I am holding the knife pointe outwards. If they all rush me at once, someone will get hur someone may die.

Riley is looking around the room, probably planning som thing, but I'm keeping an eye on him. He's a bit sneaky. That something else I may have to knock out of him. My parents nev liked sneakiness either.

'What are you going to do with us? There's no way you can lea here without getting caught. This is ridiculous. If you just let us g you can leave and this will all be over,' Beverly says, one statemer following the other in rapid succession as though she doesn't ca what she's saying, but simply hopes to get through to me.

I don't want to get into a discussion with her but she's going die, I'm certain of that. She may as well know that I'm doing th for a reason, that I deserve to be happy as well. And she needs confess. Most people confess their greatest sins before they di seeking to rid themselves of everything they have done. Bever can do that, although she will never be forgiven for stealing m child from me.

'Do you know that when my sister first came to me after I hadn't seen her for years, I didn't care about how awful she'd been when we were younger? I was filled with… something like hope. I'd felt hopeless before that because of… well, everything,' I say, waving my hands through the air. I don't want to have to explain my childhood to her, although I wonder how much she knows already. 'I thought she wanted to reconnect and that somehow we could be something like a family.'

Beverly doesn't say anything. She's watching me and watching Riley, her eyes darting between us, probably noticing that we both have the same chin and the same eyes. I share that with my sister, but the small strawberry birthmark near my eye has somehow appeared on Riley's face. When I first saw that when he was a baby, I knew it was a sign that he was meant to be mine. How he came into the world, whoever his parents were, he was mine.

'I let her stay with me whenever she needed to,' I tell Beverly, because it feels like the story needs to be told now. 'I took care of her.' My sister in a vulnerable state was not something I was used to. Her worry over the pregnancy, her anger that James wouldn't marry her, her hatred of Beverly, it all made her weak. She needed my help when she was sick with hormones and despair. I made her soup, listened to her complain. I was the perfect older sister even as my mind churned with plans for the future.

'I think you should let us go,' Beverly says. 'All of that was a long time ago and you need to let us go now.'

'So, here's the thing,' I tell her. 'I'm happy enough to let you go. I just want Riley. If he comes with me, he and I can walk out of here and you and Sam will be fine.'

I'm lying but I think it will be better if I get Riley away from her and Sam. I will take him upstairs and tell him to wait. I'm sure he'll wait for me once I get her to confess the truth. That's all I need her to do. I need her to explain so that he understands.

'Mum… no,' says Riley, a plaintive wail.

'Oh, please stop,' I say, irritated now. 'She's not your mothe Don't you understand? She's not your mother. I bet she hasn't eve told you that you have grandparents. They're interesting peopl and if you come with me, you can meet them. We'll be a prope family, Riley. I bet you want a proper family.'

'Don't listen,' says Beverly, 'it's rubbish.'

'No,' I say, looking at him, 'it's the truth, Riley. It's the absolut truth. Tell him, Beverly, tell him or I will hurt him. Tell him now I am on him in a few steps and I grab him by one of his arm holding tight, squeezing so he doesn't fight me. He tries to be the sight of the knife silences him.

She drops her head and I watch as a tear splashes onto her shoe

'Don't listen to her, Riley,' she says. 'I'm your mum.'

I feel fury rise up and I let him go. She needs to just die nov the lying bitch. I hold the knife right up to her nose. 'Tell hir the truth,' I say.

CHAPTER FORTY-EIGHT

Riley

Riley watches the woman hold the knife up to his mum and his whole body gets filled with anger. This woman is lying, she's lying, and he doesn't want to hear what she's saying anymore. And he's not going to let her hurt his mum.

Sam looks like he's about to close his eyes and die and Scotty is sitting in a corner, too scared to come near the mad woman. His stomach rumbles even though it's already filled with fear and anger. He should be home in bed by now, asleep after spaghetti for dinner, under his warm duvet with his mum in the next room, the television on and her voice repeating things from her course so she remembers them in her test. Sometimes in the night he wakes and hears her soft voice, saying the same thing again and again. He always knows he's safe then.

He should be at home and instead this woman wants to take him away from his mum and no one is doing anything because Sam is old and his mum is scared and the woman has a knife. He was scared when the knife was by his neck, but he's not scared now, now he's furious.

He opens his mouth and screams long and loud, startling everyone, even Scotty who starts barking. And in the moment of confusion and noise he launches himself at her. 'You shut up, shut up, shut up, she is my mum.'

His body collides with the woman's and she falls backwards with Riley on top of her. He can hear Scotty barking madly. He lifts his head, the woman's eyes meeting his green eyes. At the side of her left eye is a small birthmark that looks like a tiny strawberry, just like the one he has. For just a second, Riley feels like he can't hear anything at all. There is no more noise because the mark is just like the one he has. Just like he has. Just like he has. The woman has the same mark. The noise in the room comes rushing back. Sam saying, 'Stop, Scotty.' His mum shouting, 'No, Riley. Help, help us, someone, please.'

'You're…' he begins but then he feels his mother's hands grabbing for him and she pulls him off, roughly throws him toward the sofa, her movement strong like she's a big man. She looks around the room, her head going back and forth, and then she spots the hammer thing on the floor. The woman starts to sit up but his mum has the hammer thing in her hand and she stands above the woman before she can get up properly.

'He's my son,' his mum shouts and then she hits the woman with the hammer thing, 'mine,' she repeats, hitting the woman again and Riley pushes back against the sofa cushion, scared of his own mother.

Is she his mother?

CHAPTER FORTY-NINE
Heather

feel my body moving. I am being carried. There is a ringing in my ears and a tightening band of pain around my head. She hit me. The bitch actually hit me and she must have hit me hard.

I try to lift my arm to feel my head where the pain is becoming unbearable and I find that it is chained to something. How strange. I look around me but all I can see is the dark night sky and a bouncing red and blue light. She hit me. I can feel that I am being lifted and then an oxygen mask is placed over my face. I am in an ambulance because she hit me. I want to close my eyes and sleep, but I can also feel a slow burning anger. All my plans have come to nothing. I have no idea how long it will take me to get out of this ambulance, but I will have to find another way to get my child from her. She doesn't deserve him. He's mine as much as he is hers.

An image of my sister on the last day I saw her appears. I see her wild hair, sticking up and greasy with sweat and something else that I later learned was blood. I had come to the clifftop to meet her after her frantic phone call. 'He's dead, he's dead,' she had screamed down the line and I could hear that she was running.

'Who's dead? Who?' I yelled back.

'I have to find him. He's on the cliffs, I know he would be on the cliffs.'

I didn't know what she was saying. 'What? What?' I yelled, hoping to get her attention, to get her to stop running and speak to me, but then I heard a strange clunk sound and then nothing and I realised she had dropped her phone.

She was going to the cliffs instead of coming back to my apartment with the baby and that was not the plan.

The most amazing thing about my sister was that she never questioned whether or not I would be there for her. She was cruel and nasty, completely dismissive of me when we were growing up. At every opportunity she chose to laugh at me with my parents instead of stand with me against them. And yet she somehow knew, just knew, that when she came to me, I would welcome her into my life.

When I saw her standing at my door that first time, a jolt of panic went through me. Had she found out that I had been following her on Facebook? That I had set up a fake profile to keep tabs on her life? But then I looked at her and even though she was smiling, something had gone from her eyes. I stepped back to let her in, knowing that I wanted to hear what had upset her so much because her pain would give me some pleasure and, after everything I had been through, I deserved some pleasure.

She sank onto my sofa without asking if she could sit down.

'What's wrong?' I asked and she burst into tears, and I am not ashamed of the joy that coursed through me at her despair. I didn't offer her something to drink or try to comfort her. I wanted to know what had happened and then I would throw it back at her, remind her of how she had been when we were children. Then I would tell her to leave.

'I'm pregnant,' she said, 'and he won't marry me.'

I looked up at the ceiling of my apartment, contemplating its stark whiteness as I felt the whole world ripple slightly. Something had just been given to me after so much had been taken and there was never any question about what I was going to do.

'You don't need him,' I said. 'You don't need anyone but me.'

I was her complete support during her pregnancy. We both
agreed that there was no need for James and his insufferable sister
to know about me. And most importantly – no one needed to
know about the baby, except for those who already did. I told her
to stay away from doctors and hospitals. 'Babies get taken away
from mothers who don't do what they're told to do and mothers
who don't seem to be coping,' I said ominously, knowing she was
vulnerable and open to suggestion as she struggled to deal with the
idea of being a single mother. It's hard to be the centre of attention
when you have a child to take care of. I was her place of refuge,
her help. I made her lovely dinners and I let her stay overnight
whenever she wanted. I even went so far as to rub her feet when
it was near the end. And all the time I was being the most perfect
elder sister in the world, I was dreaming of the day I would hold
her baby, a baby who would carry my genetic material, in my arms.

The plan was that she would come back to my apartment with
the baby and we would leave from there.

I had talked about us raising the child together all through her
pregnancy. As James pulled away from her, I pulled her closer to me.

'You don't need to let James have access to the child. The only
people your baby needs are you and me. We'll raise him together.
We know how to raise a child and James will just interfere.'

'But he's the father,' she said. 'They won't let me just take the
baby away. James wants to be involved.' She was depressed and
whiny, huge because she retained water, no longer pretty, no
longer clever but at the mercy of her hormones and her feelings,
her ability to charm and manipulate diminished as she lay on my
sofa, crying over the man who was supposed to love her.

'He'll be a bad father if he doesn't love you. He can never love
our child because he can't love you. You know what a bad father
can do to a child,' I said, convincing her of what I knew. 'You
remember what it was like for us growing up with Dad. Mum was

horrible but he was worse. Do you want your child to be beaten
like that? Hurt like that?' I was very good. I talked her into hating
James. I managed to talk myself into hating him and I'd never
even met him, just seen his pictures on her phone – him and his
irritating little sister.

'But James is kind,' she would protest. 'He rented me an apart
ment and even though… we're not together anymore maybe he
still loves me a little bit and one day he'll want to be with me, to
be with us.'

'It's all an act,' I would reply. 'He wants to take the baby from you
and hurt him. He'll steal him away and you'll never see him again.
I wouldn't be surprised if he threw him off a cliff. Imagine that,
Georgia. He's a man. He doesn't want to take care of a baby alone.
He doesn't want to have a wife and he certainly doesn't want a child.
He'll hurt him. If he really wanted a baby, he would marry you.'

She didn't believe me but she kept coming over. She needed me
and if she was with me, she had to listen to me. His rejection of
her created a wedge of vulnerability in her psyche and I squeezed
in. And she couldn't help but be convinced.

When the baby was born, he kept telling her to go and rest but
she never did. She was afraid that if she left the baby with him he
would take or kill the child. If she was with me, I told her to rest
as well but I didn't let her sleep. I kept apologising for waking her
with stupid questions, but I made sure she stayed off balance. There
is a reason sleep deprivation is used to torture people. Georgia
became delusional, started seeing things. She thought my parents
had come to see the baby and stolen him away, she thought that
James had stolen the baby. My parents didn't know about the baby.
The only person Georgia should have been worried about was me
but she thought I was the only person she could trust. 'Don't tell
them about me,' I kept saying. 'I'm your safe place.'

She would sleep for an hour and wake in fright. James never had
the baby at night because she was still feeding him. When James

demanded that she introduce a bottle so that the baby could come
to stay with him, I knew we were running out of time.

'He's going to take him away from you,' I told her, dripping
poison into her ear. I wanted to raise the baby away from everyone, just Georgia and me, and then I would have the family I
dreamed of. There wouldn't be a father but who needed a father?
And I didn't need her either. I didn't need her at all. I wanted
to take him and run, but then she would know I had him and
everything would be revealed. I needed her to take the baby
and then I would take the baby from her. It would be as simple
and easy as that. I banked on her not pursuing me, on her just
wanting to be able to close her eyes and sleep. She took care of
the baby but she was detached from him. Georgia liked to be
the pretty centre of attention. A baby changed everything, and
not in a good way for her.

'I don't want to raise a baby by myself,' she whined. 'I'm so
tired, so tired all the time. I just want to sleep.'

'You don't have to raise him,' I told her. 'Bring him to me and
then you can go, just go and be free again. I'll take care of him. I
promise. Just don't tell James about me. I'll take him and go away
and they will never find him again.'

I saw her body relax at my words; her face shone with the
possibility of not having to take care of the needy, whiny creature.
I loved every moment with him. I fed him and changed him and
sang to him and he was mine, mine, mine. James and Georgia
were just in the way.

When she told me that James wanted to spend the afternoon
with the child and that he had booked her a hair appointment so
he could relax, I knew it was time.

'Accept the appointment. Go, get your hair done and when
you get back, he will assume that everything is fine. He'll stop
complaining about not getting time with him. And then that's
the night we leave. Bring the baby to me when he leaves and the

two of us will just disappear. We'll go somewhere lovely and rais[e] our son.'

'Our son?' she asked, bewildered and shaking her head a[s] though she wasn't sure.

'Your son, your son of course,' I replied. 'Unless you just wan[t] me to take him. I can take him, Georgia, and you can be youn[g] and beautiful again.' I watched her chin lift slightly and her cheek[s] flush as she contemplated rewinding her life to an easier time.

I repeated it over and again, told her of the places she could g[o] and the things she could do if she was not tied down to a baby.

She accepted the appointment. She went to get her hair done[,] texting me as the hours passed. *James found the bruise on his back* she texted me. *He asked about it.* The bruise was unfortunate, bu[t] I couldn't be with her all the time. Georgia never wanted a bab[y] and she grew easily weary of his crying and then her temper flare[d] and she punished him.

Never mind, I texted back. *This will all be over soon.* I imagine[d] her admiring herself in the hairdresser's mirror, my silly vai[n] sister who had no desire to look after anyone but herself. I'd ha[d] to restrain myself from hitting her when I first saw the purp[le] discolouration on his perfect skin. I hated the idea of her harmin[g] the baby that would soon be mine to take care of, but I knew [I] needed to tread carefully with her.

It was all coordinated and planned. But it's not what happene[d]. A screaming Georgia telling me that someone was dead made m[y] heart sink.

Her phone call terrified me. The fact that she was running an[d] that she had dropped her phone meant something was terrib[ly] wrong. I thought back to the things I had told her James migh[t] do to the baby. I had told her he would throw the child off th[e] cliffs to get rid of him and now she was going there. She w[as] crazier than I thought. If she had the baby with her, who kne[w] what could happen.

All that mattered was that the baby was safe. That was the only thing I cared about. As I ran to where I knew she was I worried that I had pushed her too far over the edge, that she had hurt him or something worse.

My head is pounding as that last time I saw my sister plays out in my mind. The ambulance screams through the streets, jolting me, every bump hurting my already throbbing head. My eyes are closed as the memory of that last afternoon, the last time I saw her, makes my stomach churn.

'Heart rate is rising,' I hear a man's voice say and I am drawn back to the ambulance and the shuddering ride that sends shock-waves of pain through my head. The smells of antiseptic and sweat, fear and blood make everything worse.

'Where are you taking me?' I ask, even though I can't actually see anyone. My head and neck are being held still. No one answers me and I close my eyes again and feel myself back on the cliff, the wind roaring around us and the waves crashing into the rocks below. An innocent enough place where people go to get the best Instagram photos: *#bestviewinsydney*. The grey-green rocks lead down to the deep blue sea and the colours make a fabulous backdrop for proposals. But that afternoon the wind was high, despite the spring warmth, too intense for those who value the way they look. The cliffs were empty, except for my sister.

'Georgia, Georgia,' I screamed as I saw her. There was nothing pretty left about her. She was doughy and pale, sickly looking, with heavy bags under her eyes.

'He's dead, he's dead,' she screamed when she saw me.

'Who's dead, who's dead?' I yelled back and then I saw the blue onesie in her hand, the bloodstains where the baby's chest would be. She was clutching it to herself and muttering, 'He's dead, he's dead.' I thought she meant the baby. I didn't know she meant James. I thought she had killed the baby and thrown him over the cliff. I didn't think, *No, that's impossible*, because I knew it was entirely possible. She was exhausted, depressed, hormonal and out of control. And I had encouraged all of that.

'Oh, Georgia why?' I shouted above the wind.

She looked out at the ocean where waves grew and crested and she said, 'I'm so tired, Heather. I'm just so tired.'

I stepped back away from her, horror filling my heart. The baby had been my last chance; my last chance and she had taken him from me because she never wanted me to have anything, because she was cruel and hateful and I opened my mouth and roared my pain and as I did, I ran at her. I ran at her with my hands reaching out to tear her skin like claws.

And I bumped into her, hard, with intention. And over she went.

She didn't even scream as she went down. Just accepted it.

She had loved James and he wouldn't love her back. The baby was an irritation, but she loved James and she must have lashed out at him for some reason. I will never know the full story. I didn't give her a chance to talk. Over she went and she didn't even scream on the way down.

I looked around me, frantic and panicked that I had been seen but no one was there. I couldn't think straight, couldn't breathe but I knew I needed to run.

I had done something terrible, something morally wrong. I had committed the worst of crimes and I knew that instead of the lovely life raising a child I had been dreaming of, all that waited for me were the bars of a prison and a life of torment.

I raced back to my apartment and packed a bag, grabbed whatever I needed and left. The airport was the only place I could think to go and what little money I had left was spent on a ticket to London. I couldn't think of any place further away than that.

I didn't have to leave so fast. Bodies take a while to wash up on beaches.

CHAPTER FIFTY

Beverly

'Can I please just put him to bed before I explain?' Beverly says to Constable Rivers.

They are sitting in Beverly's living room again; it's past 1 a.m. Riley's face is washed out, eyes red-rimmed, exhaustion obvious. Scotty is in his arms because Sam has been taken to hospital, his only concern was that Scotty be taken care of. He had called Liza who was frantically trying to get on a flight from Melbourne. 'I'll be fine, Liza,' Beverly heard him tell her. 'I'll explain it all when you get here.' He had handed her the phone and she had lied for him: 'Yes… he'll be fine.' She had wished, prayed that it was the truth.

Beverly is not sure Sam understands it all but then she doesn't either. She had no idea that Georgia had a sister. But now that she does, some of the pieces are falling into place.

'I want to hear too,' says Riley in a small, determined voice.

She cannot believe he is still awake. He is huddled away from her, away from who she has revealed herself to be. Not his mother. And a woman capable of great violence, but she knows that she was only capable of that because he is her son, regardless of how he was born. A mother will kill to save her child and she had been prepared to kill Heather.

But now the adrenaline that she had been running on for the last hours has disappeared, leaving her feeling the way Riley does.

She wants only to curl up in bed and have this day dissolve int the darkness of a merciful sleep.

Beverly sighs. Riley needs an explanation. He deserves one.

She reaches her hand towards him, but he pushes himself furthe back and uses Scotty as a shield – keeping her away. She has a lo of work to do to rebuild his trust. She has been lying to him h whole life. His behaviour is not surprising.

'Okay, but what you need to know first, Riley, what you nee to understand, is that your father loved you more than anythin in the world and I love you more than anything in the world.'

'But that woman was my mother? How can she be my mothe She was mad but she had the same birthmark as me, she did but sh was mad. Am I going to be mad?' He is exhausted and confuse

After Beverly had swung the mallet, every fibre of her bein alive with fury, he had cowered away from her. Sam had sat dow next to him, even as his face paled, and put his arms around th boy. Scotty kept barking and barking until she had told him t be quiet. She had looked down at the woman on the floor. Sh looked enough like Georgia that it was obvious they were relate But Georgia had never mentioned a sister, not once. Beverly kne about Georgia's abusive parents but she had no idea that there ha been anyone else in the family.

When James said Georgia was talking to someone else, th someone else was her sister. It was never another man. Her sist was going to help her raise Riley and they were simply going cut James out of his life.

Beverly had looked down at her hand and seen the mallet ther surprised that she was still holding it as she stood over Heathe prone body. She had dropped it, a soft whump filling the silen as it hit the carpet. And then she had heard the knocking on th door, pounding from upstairs. The police were there looking f her, as she had known they would be. They would have realised th they needed to return to the house and she's sure they had hea

Scotty's mad barking, Riley's scream. She had raced up the stairs to where the basement door was locked and pushed and kicked at it, shouting, 'Help!' until eventually it gave way, just as the police had found their way through the back door into Sam's house.

There had been so much shouting and she has tried to explain, but now Sam and the woman, Heather, have been taken to the hospital and Riley is next to her, cautious and disbelieving, and she tells the story again, knowing that she may very well lose her little boy. He was not hers to begin with. They had wanted her to go to the hospital as well, but she had convinced them she was fine, even as her headache made it impossible to think straight. She felt that if she left Riley alone, if he had to be with someone else tonight, she would lose him forever. The authorities would want to take him to his grandparents. Would his grandparents want him? Even if they did, she wouldn't let them. She knew what they were like. Look at the children they had produced. She pushed away any thought of Riley being like them. He was being raised by her. He had James's DNA inside him. James was kind and loyal and sweet and he hadn't deserved to die.

'You can't take him to his grandparents,' she says to the constables now, who also look haggard after their hours in the house. 'Georgia told us they were terrible people. They were abusive. You can't take him there.'

'Hold up,' says Constable Riyad. 'No one has said anything about that and anyway, we've had people checking this. Riley's other grandparents, Heather's parents, are dead, they're both dead.'

Beverly gasps. 'Dead… they're dead? But Heather said she wanted to take Riley to them. She said they would be a proper family.'

'From what we know, it was a faulty gas heater. Last winter,' says Constable Rivers. 'There was a fire.'

Beverly nods her head, a twinge of sympathy for Heather pinching at her. Heather was all alone in the world, just like she

had been before Riley. Perhaps if the woman had knocked on he
door, she would have been invited in. They could have develope
a relationship. In another life Riley's two aunts could have becom
friends.

'Why didn't she just come to see me?' asks Beverly, but sh
knows that the constables won't have the answer to this.

'And just to let you know Alexander Benton left the state th
afternoon. His son is unwell and he has gone to be with him
Constable Rivers says.

'Mr Benton? Why are you talking about Mr Benton?' Rile
asks, rubbing his red eyes.

'I thought…' Beverly says, 'I don't know what I thought.' Sh
got so many things wrong that she can't even begin to count them
She knows that she needs to start getting things right and tha
means starting with the whole truth.

'Your Uncle James is actually your father,' Beverly says to Rile
as the police watch on. 'He was my big brother and I loved hir
more than anything else in the world. He was the best huma
being I knew…'

She talks for nearly an hour, repeating herself, answerin
questions. She tries to gloss over the way James died but Rile
hears it all and her heart breaks for him. His body curls up small
and smaller on the sofa as she speaks, his eyes widening wit
incomprehension.

Beverly explains how a month after she had decided that Rile
was her son, the police came to tell her Georgia's body had bee
found. It had washed up on a beach far down the coast but
had taken time to identify her. She knows she should have fe
pity for the woman, sadness or something like that, but she w
glad. Georgia didn't deserve to be alive when James was dead. Sh
remembers feeling grateful that she would never have to fight th

woman for her child and then a heavy guilt over what she had done settled over her. But Georgia had simply disappeared and someone needed to care for Riley. That someone was her.

As she goes over everything for the constables and her son, she tries to find ways to make Riley's history easier to bear. She doesn't tell him about his hours in the house alone, just that he was here. She doesn't tell him he nearly died, just that she found him and instantly knew she had to take care of him. And when she is done and the constables have left, telling her they will be back, that more talking will be needed and statements will have to be made; she switches off the living room light and in the slight glow from the street light, she sinks onto the sofa, close enough to touch her son. But she keeps her hands to herself as she waits for him to speak.

In the weary silence, he puts Scotty on the floor and then he shuffles along the sofa and rests his head on her lap and her heart aches with the relief of his forgiveness.

'Explain it again,' he whispers.

And she does.

EPILOGUE

Ten months late[r]

Rile[y]

Riley pulls at the tie around his neck. It's tight and horrible an[d] he wants to take it off.

'Can you please leave it?' says his mum. 'I just need it to sta[y] on for the pictures.'

Riley rolls his eyes and sighs, 'Why did you have to get marrie[d] in summer?'

'Riley,' smiles his mum, 'you are nearly ten years old and abou[t] to become a big brother, you can survive a tie for another hou[r.] And it's technically autumn, not my fault we're having a heatwave[.]'

'The car is here,' says Sam. He has Scotty in his arms. Rile[y] is in charge of the old dog. He will walk him up the aisle wit[h] the two gold rings attached to his collar. Sam is giving his mu[m] away. 'I'm an honorary father today,' he keeps telling people. Li[z] and her daughters Thea and Amy are here for the wedding an[d] he and Thea have decided that they are going to see who can e[at] the most off the dessert table. 'More chocolate than you've ev[er] seen,' his mum told him.

'Let's go,' she says now and Riley gives her a thumbs up. Sh[e] looks really pretty and you can't tell she's got a baby inside h[er] yet. But he knows it's there. Her dress is long and lacy and n[ot] white but like white-pink. She has pink flowers in her hair and sh[e] doesn't look like a mum at all but she is a mum, she's his mum, and soon there will be a baby brother or sister.

They don't know what it is yet but he and Ethan had seen it on the scan and it was waving at them. He hopes it's a boy.

'A new baby means that your parents never have time for you,' Benji told him and Benji would know. He has a little brother and a little sister.

Riley was a bit worried about that. The thing is that Ethan is not his real father and his mum is actually his aunt which is a secret he's only told Benji. He got scared and angry about that for a few days until his mum shouted, 'Just what is wrong with you, Riley?' after he had thrown a glass into the sink and smashed it.

'I don't have a mum and a dad,' he had cried and then he was embarrassed because he was too old to cry like a baby. 'The new baby will have you as a mum and Ethan as a dad but I have no one and you won't want me anymore.'

His mum had grabbed him and looked at him and not let him look away. 'I am your mother. From the moment you were born I have loved you with every fibre of my being. I am your mother, Riley, and Ethan will be your father. Don't let anyone tell you any different. You're mine, my son,' she had shouted. And even though she seemed cross it hadn't mattered because the loud words went into Riley's brain and he knows it's the truth. She's his mum and a new baby won't change that at all.

Ethan told him the same thing except he didn't shout. Ethan's even going to adopt him but his mum doesn't need to adopt him because on his birth certificate it says she's his mum and some lawyer said that was okay. It's all complicated but he's not going to think about any of that today and he's especially not going to think about the bad woman who is his other aunt. He never likes to think about her.

Today all he's going to think about is the dessert table and eating chocolate with Thea and Benji, who is coming to the wedding as his special friend. That's all he's going to think about.

Beverly rests her hand on her stomach, feeling the tiny little bubbles that will one day become fierce kicks. The baby has only just started moving. She's not even showing and is still fitting into her jeans, but she can't wait for a huge bump and arms and legs pushing everywhere.

'Ready to go, love?' asks Sam and she nods, taking a quick look in the mirror to make sure she doesn't have lipstick on her teeth. It won't be a large wedding, just fifty people, but all the people coming mean the world to her and Ethan. Ellie has already left in the first car, her bridesmaid's dress a bright yellow. 'I'm dressed in sunshine,' she crowed as she looked at herself in the mirror, making Riley and Beverly laugh.

A week after everything had happened, on the first day Riley wanted to go back to school, she had gone to the hospital to see Ethan and apologise. She hadn't resisted when he opened his arms for a hug, his cast heavy and stubble dotted along his jawline.

She had stayed for two hours, explaining what had happened, starting at the very beginning.

'But why didn't you just explain?' he kept saying.

'I essentially stole a child, Ethan. At the time his grandparents were alive. He would have been sent to live with them. I was only eighteen. I was worried about getting caught every day of his life, but I had no idea about Heather.'

She felt lighter as she spoke to him, as though she weren't so tightly bound to the earth, held down by her secrets. Every time she told someone the story; more weight lifted off her. Marie had listened to her tale in silence and when Beverly was done, she had stood up from her desk and filled the kettle and then she had opened a small cupboard where she stored her personal things and taken out a packet of expensive chocolates. 'I think we need a good sugar hit after that,' she said, smiling. Beverly had sighed, relieved at Marie's lack of judgement. 'If you had told me, I could have helped more,' the older woman told her. 'People mostly just want to help; you should remember that.' Beverly had moved to Marie to hug her. 'I'll remember that,' she said.

In the hospital, Ethan had shifted in his bed as she spoke and when she was finished, she believed that at least she had given him closure. He could look back at their relationship and understand that their break-up had nothing to do with what he had or had not done.

'Can we start again?' he asked her when she got up to leave.

'After everything you know, you still want to be with me?' she had asked, incredulous even as her heart lifted at the idea.

'Bev, you did it out of love for him. Whatever you did wrong, it was out of love for James and Riley. Of course I want to be with you.'

She hadn't been able to resist climbing onto the hospital bed so she could lie next to him and hold him. And when he had been discharged, he had come home to her little house and been cared for by her and Riley, his parents and sister popping in and out during the day. 'I wanted to call you and tell you he was in the hospital,' Ethan's sister Fiona told her, 'but he said to give you some space and time to think. He didn't want you back in his life out of sympathy.' She and Fiona are becoming better friends every day.

When Ethan stayed with her, Beverly would return home from work and find soup in the fridge or the washing done. The house seemed warmer, despite the cold months, and Beverly experienced moments of feeling part of a family, a family she would now be permanently and officially part of.

Beverly and Riley and Sam climb into the old black Rolls Royce with a white satin ribbon tied to its bonnet. She cannot wipe the smile off her face.

'We're going to be a proper family now,' says Riley.

'You always were a family, Riley,' says Sam. 'Family is about love and care and that's what you've always had.'

'Oh, Sam,' says Beverly, her eyes tearing up.

'Now, now, Beverly, don't ruin your pretty make-up. My Marjorie would say you look a treat and you do. She would tell you to enjoy every moment. That's exactly what Marjorie would do.'

Beverly laughs, 'Then that's what I'll do. That's exactly what I'll do.'

Heather

'Another letter to your son?' the nurse asks as I push the envelope over the counter.

'Yes, he loves me writing to him,' I say. The nurse smiles. She has a small piece of something caught between her front teeth and I think about telling her but don't.

I return to my room where I am writing in my journal, as Dr Kundera told me to do every day. Mostly I write about what Ben and I will do when I am free to do as I please. Dr Kundera has assured me that I am making excellent progress and that soon I will be able to walk out of here and go and see Ben and explain that Beverly is not his mother. Once it's all explained he will come away with me. She calls him Riley but I'm sure that he won't mind changing his name to Ben. He is more of a Ben in my opinion.

I am sorry that he won't be able to meet my parents. Their deaths were a tragic accident, a leaking gas heater that led to a terrible fire. Dr Kundera explained what happened over and again because I couldn't believe it at first. I didn't tell him I was there on the night the heater leaked gas into the air and then suddenly caught fire. There's no need for him to know about that.

Sometimes I think of them burning and my whole body breaks out in a sweat even as I shiver. Dr Kundera told me that they were dead before the fire started, so that's something, I suppose. I don't like to think of them in pain despite how they raised my sister and me. I knew that gas heater was trouble, and that the pipe was easily pulled so that it would leak through the house, making sur they slept as the fire started. A really tragic accident.

I have decided to forgive my parents for the way they raise me, and to forgive Georgia for the way she treated me and fc making me think Ben was dead. I'll even forgive Beverly once m son and I are together.

I believe that forgiveness is the way forward for Ben and me And this time I have a proper plan on how to make sure he finally mine. This time I will engage lawyers and the police onc I've taken him from Beverly and her terrible influence. Onc everyone knows the truth, I'm sure that Ben will be mine foreve

I just have to get out of here and then my whole life will b different.

The first place I'm going to take Ben is the zoo. I'm sure he'll lo that, I write.

Outside it's warm despite it being autumn. I'll be allowed m walk in the garden soon. I try to stay away from the other residen here because some of them seem a little delusional. One day I wi tell Ben all about my time here, one day. Dr Kundera refuses t give me a timeline for my release, but that's fine. I won't be he much longer. A mother needs to be with her child and I kee explaining that to whoever will listen.

I need to be with my son and soon enough, I will be.

The second place I will take Ben… I write.

A LETTER FROM NICOLE

Hello,

I would like to thank you for taking the time to read *The Mother's Fault*. If you did enjoy it, and want to keep up to date with all my latest releases, just sign up at the following link. Your email address will never be shared and you can unsubscribe at any time.

www.bookouture.com/nicole-trope

Sometimes a book takes a while to find a life of its own, to really feel like the story is going somewhere, but that wasn't the case with this novel. I remember thinking, *I've only just begun and yet it's already finished*. It felt like the story wanted to be in the world.

I hope you have enjoyed Riley and Beverly's story and that you feel some sympathy for Georgia and even Heather. People don't begin their lives as monsters. They have to be turned into monsters by time and circumstance.

All these characters were so clear to me from the very beginning and I can see Riley and Benji now, sitting on top of the monkey bars in the sunshine, discussing all the changes that have happened in Riley's life. He's going to grow up into a wonderful young man and he is going to be the best big brother.

I loved writing the Epilogue to this novel, especially from the perspective of Heather who is still hoping to get her son back one day, despite everything. She is an interesting but chilling character.

If you have enjoyed this novel, it would be wonderful if yo
could take the time to leave a review. I read them all and reall
enjoy hearing your thoughts.

If you'd like to ask a question or let me know you liked thi
novel, you can find me on Facebook and Twitter and I'm alway
happy to connect with readers.

Thanks again for reading
Nicole x

NicoleTrope

@nicoletrope

ACKNOWLEDGEMENTS

I always begin by thanking Christina Demosthenous for her insightful editing, unwavering support and for making me feel that she is always available for any concerns I have. I am learning so much from her with each new book and have her voice guiding my work every day.

I would also like to thank Sarah Hardy for her work in publicity, spreading the word and getting the novel all over the internet. Thank you to Lucy Cowie for the copyedit and Liz Hatherell for the proofread. I have to include the whole team at Bookouture, including Alexandra Holmes, Martina Arzu, Alba Proko – who takes care of audio rights – and Lisa Brewster for the eye-catching cover.

A big thank you to my mother, Hilary. It's not easy to read a novel when you know someone is waiting for your opinion but you manage it in record time and then you still do the final proofread with me. Thank you for taking every sentence so seriously and making sure I get it right.

Thanks to my family who applaud each new book, and especially to Isabella who reads them all and accuses me of keeping her up at night.

And, of course, to those who love to read as much as I love to read. Thanks for reading what I write.